D1225644

Also by Martin Murie

Losing Solitude
Windswept
Burt's Way
Red Tree Mouse Chronicles
Seriously Insistent

BREAKOUT

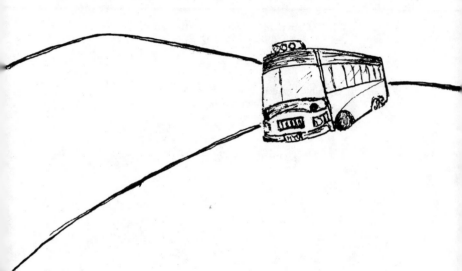

MARTIN MURIE

PACKRAT BOOKS

PRINTED IN
THE UNITED STATES OF AMERICA
This novel has been granted powerful aid along the way. The Center
for Biodiversity gave generously from its expertise and rich fund of
documentary material regarding endangered species.
Special thanks to Ronnie Francisco, Director of Admissions, Friends
care Center, Yellow Springs, Ohio, for showing me that a home for
the elders can be just that, a home. And to Alison Murie, Raven
Murie, Mark DeLozier and Mary Scriver, heartfelt thanks for your
patience and no-nonsense critiques. All errors are mine.

Copyright © 2005 by Martin Murie
ISBN 0-9702922-3-6

Printed on acid-free paper by Industrial Press
Malone, New York

Published by

Packrat Books
North Bangor, New York

I think I could turn and live awhile with the animals, they are so placid and self-contained.

I stand and look at them sometimes half the day long.

They do not sweat and whine about their condition.

* * *

Not one is respectable or unhappy over the whole earth.

So they show thier relations to me and I accept them.

They bring me tokens of myself—they evince them plainly in their possession.

I do not know where they got those tokens, I must have passed that way untold times ago and negligently dropt them…

Walt Whitman. Song of Myself

NOTE TO THE READER

Sketches of animals and plants, marking breaks in the narrative, include a few of the many species highly endangered or nearly extinct.

Kingston, New York.

Rufus Knutson was frying an egg when the phone rang. He hooked a foot around a kitchen chair and pulled it to the end of the counter and picked up. It was Jennifer.

"Hi Jennifer, how you doing?"

"Pretty good, working at the ferret lab, getting the hang of it."

"Good. You hear from Wayne?"

"A postcard, that's all. No return address. You'd think he could have...oh, never mind. Reason I'm calling is Enid and I think it's high time we three have a meeting, get this endangered species outfit up and running."

There was a sizzling sound from the stove, the egg destroying itself, but Rufus was focused elsewhere. "Jennifer, what was the postmark on that postcard?"

"Greybull. He said he might go look into the endangered red squirrel situation. That's about all he said."

"All right, that's good. He'd have made it to Greybull the same day he left Medicine Bow and then he took the trouble to buy a postcard and a stamp and write you a few words. Picture postcard?"

"Wild horses. Why all this curiosity about a stupid postcard? Like you were a detective or something. You think something's happened to Wayne."

Smoke was rising from the frying pan. "Hold on a second." He put the phone down and turned off the burner and tried to dump the egg onto his plate, but it was stuck to the pan, smoke still rising. Rufus grabbed the spatula, scraped the egg free, all the while thinking about Wayne, and the catch in Jennifer's voice. He returned to the phone. "Sorry, had to turn off the stove."

"I've called at a bad time."

"No problem. So, where were we?"

"I was asking for a meeting. Endangered species."

"Uh huh."

"Rufus, I worry about Wayne."

"I do too. Reason is he's a dumb, stubborn ox, won't admit he's totally...well, you know this...he's in love."

"No I do not know this."

"Yes you do. You're as bad as he is. None of my business, but I made it my business, back there in Wyoming. I told Wayne from the get-go he'd fallen for you. I tried to get him to face reality, but he'd already put up a big seven-foot buffalo fence of denial."

"Rufus, you're stepping over a line here."

"Yup. Before I crawl back, I better tell you that seven-foot fence was Wayne's knowing you were a scientist and he was a mechanic from Montana. I saw through all that. Didn't dare mention it to him. Should have."

"Are you finished?"

"Yup. And I'm sorry."

"You're not sorry at all, goddamn you...and thank you. I put up a fence too."

"You sure did."

"There's no reason to tell any of this to Enid."

Rufus laughed and that started a coughing fit, from the smoke that filled the room. His eyes watered. "Jennifer, Enid's no dummy."

"Oh."

"How is she?"

"She's okay, rented a place in Rock River. She's impatient, so am I. We want to actually do something, go on the offensive."

"Okay, why don't you and Enid talk it over, then we can talk on the phone."

"No. No can do. Enid and I have talked it over, and over and over and we get nowhere."

"Hmmm. Well, to be honest with you, at my age it's awfully late to start something new."

"Listen to me, Rufus, it's not something new, it's something going on, from out of the hell we all went through out here. You can't quit now."

He was looking at the bounds of his tiny kitchen, remembering mountains. Treacherous, fascinating, a continent away.

"Rufus, you still there?"

"Yup."

"I'm asking you to fly out here, like, day after tomorrow."

He heard in the phone's hum the howl of Wyoming wind, but Jennifer's words were there too, her refusal to make allowances for his age. Neither had Wayne."

"Where do we meet?"

"Medicine Bow? Virginian Hotel?"

"I'll catch me a plane."

Virginian Hotel, Medicine Bow, Wyoming.

Jennifer Felway rattled the ice in her glass and plunked it down hard on the table. "If Rufus doesn't show up soon I'm having another."

Jennifer's colleague, Enid Shaw, was watching a pair of tourists work their way along the left hand wall of the bar room, studying the line of portraits of bad men of the west. Butch Cassidy was there, and Tom Horn, Kid Curry and The Sundance Kid and lots more. "The money accounts are all set up," she said, as of this afternoon. Three banks, actually. Two in Cheyenne, one in Laramie."

"Good. Let's call that step number one, but money doesn't go out all by its lonesome and do what has to be done."

Enid turned away from the tourists. "We can't save endangered species by simply doing what the other enviro people are doing. Remember? We said that at the start, swore we'd do something big, something with life in it."

Jennifer stared at her glass, turned it slowly. "Life, yes. Liveliness. That was the idea. We were going to go to the roots of disaster."

"And raise some hell," Enid smiled, shook her head, tossed off the rest of her drink. "Rufus, where are you when we need you?"

A lean man in tight jeans and plaid shirt came in from the restaurant. He did a double take. "Jennifer, you still around?"

"Can't stay away. How're you, Jeff?" They shook hands. "Enid, this is Jeff Corrigan. Jeff, my friend Enid Shaw."

"Heard about you, ma'am. You cut quite a figure a while back." He laughed, tugged at his silver-buckled belt, winked at Jennifer, "Where's that biker friend of yours?"

"He sent a card from Greybull." She turned to Enid. "Jeff's a veterinarian, does everything from cranky horses to broken-wing hawks. He charms them all."

The veterinarian took that as an invitation to sit down. "Been hearing rumors."

"I know."

"Yeah, you do know, don't you. So, I have to ask, is it true you got one hell of a lot of money from those corporations?"

"Quite a lot," Enid said. "Not for us, it's in the form of a grant, for a specific purpose."

"Specific purpose. Right, I'm all ears." He tapped the lobe of his right ear.

Jennifer said, "A fund to save at-risk organisms from extinction.

"And that would include us seriously up-the-creek Homo saps?"

"I suppose it ought to," Enid said.

"Believe it or not, ladies, I've been giving that some thought lately. Nothing's going right for us citizens. When I was a kid, up in Sublette County…oh hell, never mind that…hey, good to see you, both of you." He got up, cocked his head, gave them a thumbs up and drifted off, smiling, greeting people. He knew everyone, it seemed, tourists excepted.

Jennifer stood up, waving wildly. "Rufus, over here." Enid rose and went to him and gave him a hearty bear hug, held it, murmured, "Rufus, it seems like ages." Her eyes were wet. Jennifer grabbed him too, lightly, asked about his flight and the long delay.

"They held the Casper flight in Salt Lake, fixing the wing or something."

"Terrorist scare?"

He shrugged.

Jennifer caught the bartender's eye.

Enid was thinking that it would be hard to put together three more different personalities: Rufus, a loner from way back, shy of personal entanglements; Jennifer, skilled molecular biologist, rebel and renegade; Enid, daughter of privilege, adept at upscale social graces, dodges, obediences, only recently adrift from all of that, wondering who she really is.

Rufus, worn out from a long day's passivity, drifted on the blend of voices, responded absently to the bartender. "Double shot."

Enid inquired about Otis.

"Same as ever. He's got some ideas on this species thing."

Jennifer said, "We have to get Otis on board."

"I'm all for that. How about him taking my place?"

Jennifer hammered the table. "NO."

Enid said, calmly, decisively, "That's not in the cards."

The drinks came. They touched glasses. Rufus said, "Otis can shake things up. Are you ready for that?"

Enid laughed softly. "Don't try to scare us, Rufus. Yes, we're ready."

"He thinks this endangered species thing is a typical middle class, top-down operation. For that reason alone the odds are against it."

Enid nodded, smiling. "And does he have a suggestion as to how we can turn ourselves inside out?"

Rufus took a hefty nip of whiskey, chased it, glanced around, chuckled silently to himself, remembering the vigorous and enjoyable discussion he and Otis had indulged in. It had become an event in the Maple View social room. Other residents, those who were alert enough, perhaps a third of those present, noticed the two men tapping their coffee mugs on the metal table top, their shakings of heads, their flailing hands. And a tall woman who liked to dress in long satiny gowns and who had a voice like a bass viol, maneuvering among the tables and wheelchairs and walkers to join the discussion, making Otis even happier. Otis loved disputation. Rufus had a lesser hankering for it, but he'd found that a good argument made a stir in days that dragged in bland emptiness, especially lately, his second year of widowerhood.

Jennifer said, "We're waiting."

"Okay. After Otis dropped that little putdown, he said this whatever it is...don't we have a name for it yet?"

"No, and that's a big error," Jennifer said. "A name would point us in the right direction. Well, what did Otis say?"

"Spend money, don't raise money."

"Lovely," Jennifer said.

Enid said, "There is a certain seductive attractiveness about that. I've been having this nagging thought, that we're too late. Species can't wait while we get into gear, fund-raising and all that." She sighed and looked away and spoke as if musing to herself. "In truth, if we face up to it, we're very likely past the point of recovery. Apocalypse."

Rufus said, "That's the word Maud used."

"Maud?"

"At Maple View. She barged into our discussion. Otis tells me Maud lost her husband in Korea, raised two sons and now the sons have their own families and the whole bunch of them are below poverty level and one of them looking to the military for a job."

"Apocalypse," Jennifer said, "thousands of organisms going under, as we speak. So, about money, I'd say if somebody wants to give us a bunch of it, no strings attached, we don't turn them down. Meanwhile, let's spend like crazy."

"Agreed then," Enid said, noticing the quick glances between her two compadres. She read them easily: amusement, her managerial style, natural to a woman married to a corporate lawyer. Enid let it pass, because much had happened to her in Rock River in the last few days of idleness and loneliness. She had decided to shuck off a lot of baggage. She was what life had made her; she'd go with that, not enough time for a rehab. She said, "I'm sure Otis has other suggestions."

Rufus smiled. "Otis never runs out of ideas. Here's one he kept hammering on: terrible waste of time to keep trudging along the dusty old road to Damascus discovering the wisdom of nature, and come back and tell us about it, and tell us and tell us, how *the ecology* will save us all; soul shift, neat 12-step organic instructions in plastic wrappers. Talk, tons of talk. Where has it gotten us? He says it's way past time to break out of all that, break out of these simple notions in feel-good packages. On and on like that. I got sick of it, told him so. Maud told him too; she said, "Hey, we got the point way last week so shut the hell up.""

Again Jennifer banged on the table. Enid, startled, spilled a few drops of her drink. Recovering, she found herself marvelling, with a dash of envy, at Jennifer's youthful vibrancy.

"Breakout," Jennifer was saying, "there's our NAME. Let's go to back of beyond, plough a fresh furrow. BREAKOUT. Ho hoh and jolly ho."

Enid, looked at Rufus. "I like it."

Rufus said, "Yup, it'll do."

At the bar Jeff the vet was talking to Jasper Durgan, owner of Antlers Motel. Jennifer's outburst caught their attention. "Those women are in for rough times," Jeff remarked. "Wonder if they know it."

Durgan disagreed. "I wouldn't call milking the corporations for all that money such a rough row to hoe."

"Problem is, the money's tied up in a do-good project to save endangered critters."

"Be nice if they'd do us some good while they're at it, put Medicine Bow on the map."

Jeff smiled. "They just might do that very thing. Imagine, working out of a state like Wyoming, for god sake, on a campaign like that. Who's the gant old coot with them?"

"Rufus Knutson. He and that biker, Wayne, stayed at The Antlers. You know, Jeff, I sort of sided with them when they went up against the pharmas. I don't especially want that spread around."

"Good god, Jasper, everybody in Carbon county knows about you being a mite friendly to them. Lots of people were. Hasn't harmed your business any, has it?"

"What's harmed my business is not enough dudes coming through here looking for a bed and coffee and danish at seven in the A.M."

"Everybody knows that too. I wonder how the Virginian's doing."

"Better than me, that's for sure."

The Breakout trio adjourned to the dining room, where they talked about old times, putting off further difficult probes of the future.

They agreed to meet again, next day. Rufus retired to one of the Virginian's ornate Victorian hotel rooms that had been reserved for him. The bill would go to Breakout. Jennifer and Enid drove toward Rock River. The night was black, sprinkled with stars, and mild. They were silent until Enid asked. "Breakout to where?"

Jennifer said, "I haven't the faintest idea."

Rock River, Wyoming.

Enid Shaw stood under a spectacular cottonwood that spread its arms over the highway's shoulder. A few of the cottonwood's leaves, guided by the wind, scratched the weathered clapboards of an abandoned false-fronted building.

Enid had stopped to study the panes of glass in its window. She counted them. Twelve. She leaned closer. The glass was from a time when glass was not rolled smooth. In a fine patina of dust Enid's face glowered, one eye larger than the other and the mouth looked like a cracked walnut. She drew back. What am I doing here, all alone?

Rock River, middle of nowhere? A few streets intersecting U.S. 30, each street two or three blocks long. That was it. A flagpole held the stars and stripes and Wyoming's white buffalo on blue. Lower, in a window, a Coors neon sign and over the doorway a weathered slab of wood named the place: STEGOSAURUS BAR. A lone pickup sat in front.

Lightning streaked across high cumulus approaching from the west, their roiling tops brilliantly lit, their bottoms dark.

Enid walked to the next corner. Two houses down the street a heavy stoop-shouldered man in overalls and a young man, hardly more than a boy, worked with squared-off stone.They were putting a stone front on a wheelchair access ramp. The stones were a conglomerate, pale pink, deep rose, specks of black. Enid walked that way and stood still and watched, appreciating the casual-seeming way the man slid mortar into place with one slick motion of the trowel. The younger man noticed Enid, murmured something. The man with the trowel used its handle to give a final tap on stone, knocked down a dab of stray mortar, turned to Enid and raised heavy white brows.

"I'm just curious," Enid said.

The man nodded. "We're trying to beat the rain." Lightning zigged again, thunder followed.

"You're experts," Enid said.

"I am, he's hopin' to be."

Enid made a bold guess. "Father and son."

The dad nodded, the son trundled the wheelbarrow to a pile of stones at the back end of a dump truck.

Enid stepped closer, into the shadow of the building's generous eaves. "What do you think about endangered species?"

The master mason reached for another stone, changed his mind, faced her. "You're lookin' at one."

"Oh?"

"It's all pours nowdays; they slap up forms, call in the truck and pour. Sometimes they glue on fake faces."

The son dumped the wheelbarrow. "Dad, I'll finish."

Enid turned to go. "Didn't mean to slow you down."

"No problem." He handed the trowel to his son. "Don't skimp on mortar, let's use it up."

Rain came in a furious assault on earth, pavements, buildings, vehicles and flags. The master mason flipped a canvas over the unfinished work and his son tossed a few stones to secure the canvas's edges, all in half a minute at most. They joined Enid beneath the eaves. The storm shifted to a hurl of small hailstones and cold air.

"Like somebody opened a goddamn freeze locker," the son said.

Casper, Wyoming.

Rufus parked the rental at the airport. He opened the door, but didn't get out. He sat there in the heat, his thoughts drifting back to the meetings with Enid and Jennifer. They'd come up with a "phase one" plan for Breakout, but now in broad daylight the plan looked pale. He contemplated going into the terminal to stand in lines with cell phone people and wait for the privilege of sitting cramped and helpless thousands of feet above the earth in the slow hands of time and whatever chance might deliver. And arrive at his apartment in Kingston, fetch the cat from the family downstairs, go to McDonald's for coffee and danish, read the paper. Then what?

His bad hip sent a complaining twinge. Useless old dog. He heaved himself into the full glare of the day. "Hell with it." He went to the Hertz office, rearranged the rental's contract, picked up a free map of the city and the state. He drove off, found Wyoming 220 and turned west.

P hoenix, Arizona.

Dear Jennifer,

Hanging out here with a couple bikers, one of them we call Red wants to be a journalist. So far his job is copy proofing at the local paper. He's been keeping track of the Mount Graham red squirrel situation.

My job here ends soon, when the guy I'm replacing gets back from vacation. The heat is terrible. I miss Wyoming and Medicine Bow. Miss you too.

Your friend,

Wayne

K ingston. Maple View Nursing Home.

Otis Rameau picked up the phone, heard Jennifer's voice and was pleasedd, but answered in his normal curmudgeonly manner. Yes, he had received her Leanin' Tree post card and appreciated it very much, had it propped on his bedside table.

"Those Leanin' Tree cards are hard to find these days," Jennifer said. "I understand the artist has retired."

"Ah. Well then, I have a collector's item." He was looking at the card as they spoke: a colorful canyon, on the edge of which a grizzled old cowboy hung upside down, one spur hooked into a small bush at the very edge of the drop-off, his Stetson twirling into blue depths, his horse wild-eyed on the very brink while a vulture on a naked tree cocked its head knowingly. At a convenient ledge a coiled rattlesnake met the man's gaze, eyeball-to-eyeball.

Jennifer said, "The reason I'm calling is to ask you to be on the board of Breakout."

"Breakout?"

"The endangered species outfit. Enid and Rufus and I got together at the Virginian, talked about it, decided to name it *Breakout*. Your comments to Rufus, by the way, triggered that decision. Do you like the name?"

Otis thought about it. "Couldn't be better," he said, and now his voice was warmly human. "However," he added, "as for being on the board, I'll have to remind you I'm an inmate of a nursing home."

"No problem," she said. "You're an experienced person with a background in activism, and a lively mind. That's why we're asking you, please, join us."

Otis replied in a non-commital manner, but Jennifer could tell by his tone that it was pro forma talk. Without actually saying so, he was agreeing to be on the board. Jennifer brought him up to date. Enid had moved from the motel in Rock River, had rented a house there and installed a computer. That would be Breakout headquarters, at least for now. And she had hired a web master in Laramie and set up a Breakout listserv."

At that point, Otis couldn't help mentioning Maple View's Mac Quadra, a dinosaur, slow download, long waits for access, even though only a handful of inmates used it. Not everyone confined to a nursing home deserved to be written off as incompetent and in a stupor with no hankering to keep in touch with the world outside the walls. Otis went on at length, Jennifer listened. Then she, taking a cue from Enid's decisive style, and catering to the decision to spend money big time, proposed that Breakout buy a computer, donate it to Maple View with the proviso that someone there monitor the Breakout web site and listserv. "What model?" she asked.

"State of the art," he said.

Sybille canyon, Wyoming.

Dear Wayne,

Thanks so much for your letter. My new job at the ferret lab is demanding, but so far I like it. There are three of us: physiologist, ethologist and me. The Wyoming toad colony is doing well; the ferrets take a lot of careful management. But that's what we're here for. Next month we hope to release another batch of ferrets into the wild. I'm looking forward to that.

You might remember the location of Sybille canyon, northeast of Rock River. Isolated and beautiful. Tourists stop from time to time.

The big news is that Enid, Rufus, Otis and I have started the endangered species enterprise. The listserv is BREAK-OUT@LISTSERV.SPEAKUP.ORG

The web site is >www.endangered.org<

So, pass the word. Really loved getting your letter. Please write again, and often.

Your friend,

Jennifer.

Distant mountains, vistas with a far reach that after a while turned monotonous. Rufus turned on the radio, surfed, switched off. Independence Rock looked too much like a tourist site; he passed it by, but now, on the right, a turn-off and a place to park, next to a monster motor home and a car with house trailer attached. In the near distance a great rock, miniature mountain range carved by eons of weather into clefts, arroyos, overhangs.

A couple of sparrows flitted through nearby sage and pale sweeps of ripe grass. Rufus reached for his binoculars, roved until he caught one of the sparrows long enough to note tint of bill, head striping and shape of tail, but didn't worry about species identity; maybe he'd look it up in Peterson, later, maybe not. Suddenly the great rock filled his view field, and he noticed little figures, humans climbing. He lowered the binocs. Five people up there, each of them choosing an individual route. More huge rock upthrusts, even bigger, crowded the skyline. He took the trail to the base of the rock and climbed. The surfaces were rough, making for easy traction. He stopped once to catch his breath. A raven flew over. He watched it cross a wide expanse of dull mid-day sage. He climbed further, squeezed through a narrow passage that opened onto a shallow pool of still water. He levered himself down, touched the water. It was warm. He stayed still, stared through the perfectly transparent lens of water to the grainy bottom. A small hard-shell water beetle scooted into and out of view. Rufus reversed the binocs, looked through one eyepiece into a universe, tiny critters scooting here and there. At least two different species. He thought about their life spans. Did a minute equal a day, for them, for their unconscious selves? Their bodies? No need to know.

There were dead ones too. and little jungles of stuff that wind and rain and snowmelt must have drifted into the pool, enough to set up an ecosystem. The little jungles made patterns, like continents on a map. Out of the corner of an eye he caught a quick slither on dry rock at the pool's edge. Lizard.

Climbing down with care, taking a different route, he came close to a drop-off where two swallows roved back and forth. Forked tails, bodies white below, irridescent purple-green above. Rufus breathed deeply, stretched, wondered if he'd ever felt so free, so irresponsible. He said, "They grace the rock."

"What'?"

Rufus turned, faced a man in shirtsleeves and shorts, legs and face tanned, hair mostly gray and cut in a stiff marine brush. A woman, further down, was being very careful in her descent.

"Violet-green swallows," Rufus said. "I had this notion, that they grace the rock."

The man came close, leaned toward the drop-off. "Amazing grace?"

"I doubt it. Those birds are on their own."

"Yeah, I guess you're right." He drew back. "Heights bother me."

"Me too."

"Have a good day."

"You too."

The man joined the woman and they made their way to the motor home.

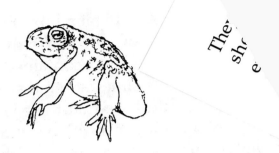

Maple View, New York.

Herb Swanson had very little use for Otis Rameau. The feeling was mutual. They didn't know each other at all well. Otis had only an animal sense of danger, the way Herb looked at a person, wide-eyed and ready. And Herb felt a cold chill of resentment whenever he faced what he took to be smug judgementalism lurking in Otis's mild gaze.

The Maple View computer sat in a corner of the social room, near the doorway that opened on the concrete slab bordered by low shrubs known as the patio. It was here that Herb and Otis and the other computer users had come into serious conflict. They resolved it with a pact, a strict parceling of times on line to which they all adhered with spartan rigor.

Three days after Jennifer's phone talk with Otis, two men in logoed coveralls showed up in the delivery entrance with two big cartons on a dolly which they trundled into the social room.

25

opened the bigger box. From a profuse shower of styrofoam puffballs a computer emerged. The other box contained a laser printer. The halt and the lame gathered around, watched, amazed. Could it be that their HMO chain had been monitoring conditions and from a deep well of compassion determined that Maple View deserved a second computer? Heavy users like Maud and Herb and Sylvie and Otis couldn't take that seriously. There must be another explanation. There was. Herb was the first to know. He confronted Otis. "You got any idea about this?"

"I do," Otis said. "I meant it to be a surprise."

"It was," Herb conceded, keeping his hard gaze on Otis. "Well, you going to tell me?"

"It's a gift, from Breakout."

"And what, pray tell, is that?"

Otis repeated, nearly word for word, the Statement of Intent that Jennifer had written for the listserv. "Breakout is a space for discussion about plants and animals that are at risk of extinction. It's a free speech space. There is only one rule: Generalities and speculation should arise from factual information or by direct experience with the organisms themselves. Let the dialogue begin."

"Well," Herb said, "ain't that a beautiful bunch of high flying words. Now, if you don't mind,

let's get down to the bottom line. Th
you cooked up with that bird ᵥ
yours. I've seen him hanging ar₍
quite a lot, can't recall his name."

Otis nodded, stiffly. "His name is Rufuꜱ,
yes, he's in on Breakout, along with a few others,
me included, but don't let it spoil your beauty
sleep, Herb. The point is, this computer is for all
of us to use."

"Except when you're using it. You'll be on it a
hell of a lot of the time."

"I'll set up a schedule. Anybody can sign up."

They looked acrosss the social room at the new
computer. "No," Herb said, "*We* is the operative
word. *WE* will be setting up the schedule.
Democratic decision."

Otis glared, but stayed cool enough. "All right,
let's do it."

Herb shifted his cane from one knobbled hand
to the other, leaned heavily forward. "I don't
know what all went down out there in Montana
…"

"Wyoming,"

"Wherever. A lot of money changed hands and
there were murders."

"Accidental deaths."

ho's to know? The whole thing was hushed

"The corporations did that, covering their asses. Nothing to do with me, or my good friend Rufus."

"Breakout. I wouldn't mind breaking out of here, and I don't care who knows it. Stuck myself in here on account of my daughter-in-law. We fought, I lost. That's the size of it." He limped away.

It took Otis a good half hour to merge his instincts with those of the new computer. From a nearby table Herb and Maud watched like hungry falcons. At the coffee urns, Sylvie sipped de-caf from her own colorful cup, quietly impatient, knowing that she could be doing a quicker job of it. She was a digital natural. For her, Maple View's creaky old Mac would usually roll over and wag tail. There had been times when both Herb and Otis had received help from her, even though each of them still had trouble teasing her name from their forgettery.

Otis got up from the keyboard. "It's all yours, Maud. I left Breakout's listserv instructions on the screen in case you're interested."

Herb went to his room, tried to read, returned to the social room and watched Maud until her time ran out. She rose reluctantly and somewhat majestically. "It's a darling, Herb. I joined that Breakout list, left their latest post for you."

Herb said, "I suppose I ought to join too, see what they're up to."

"We owe them that courtesy," Maud said.

Herb sat and looked at the screen.

To: BREAKOUT@LISTSERV.SPEAKUP.ORG

From: annbr@wyoming.com

Re: Jumping mouse

I live in Chugwater, Wyoming. I got curious about this threatened Jumping Mouse, /Zapus hudsonius preblei/. The U.S. Fish and Wildlife has put out maps showing areas where the mouse is to be protected.

Cubin, our representative in Congress, says this particular mouse hasn't even been proven to live in Wyoming grasslands. I've talked to a Bureau of Land Management biologist, told him I want to see one of those mice. He might contact people in U.S. Fish and Wildlife, or state Fish and Game, about live trapping a mouse.

Cubin says that in order to determine whether a Zapus is of the sub-species to be protected is actually a 'preblei" one has to kill it and boil it and take careful measurements of its teeth. Really?

Anna

Disappointed, Herb read it twice. His basic supposition that the Breakout caper would be the usual enviro blah-blah was supported to a degree or two by the Zapus posting, but he had expected something more flagrant. This mouse, pretty mild. Who gave a damn one way or another about some species nobody ever heard of, a mouse so much like some other mouse that it has to be boiled to find its name. It's all politics, as usual, he decided. He set up his own mail program and then stalled on inventing a password. Remembering the damn thing was the problem. He sat there a while, hands on keyboard, aware that Sylvie was waiting her turn. Finally, he typed *Zapus*.

Sybille canyon, Wyoming.

A warm July day, cumulus building above canyon walls, the dashing little creek racketing behind the lab buildings. Enid was meeting Jennifer's two colleagues. The conversation was lively, youthful and pungent, careening easily into aspects of biology that didn't appear very often in Enid's collection of bird guides. She would have preferred to remain ignorant of cannibalism in the animal world, of lampreys sucking sustenance from the flesh of other fishes, mad cow prions, whirling disease in trout, exotic insects endangering native trees. Steve noticed Enid's blank look. "Enough shop talk," he said. "Enid, tell us about Breakout."

She told them that Breakout was only a squalling baby at this point, but there was a web site and a listserv. "We do want to try new approaches."

Lisa and Steve nodded politely, but Lisa said, "With all the very best wishes in the world for Breakout's success, I have to admit I'm kinda numb by this time. So many environmental campaigns and writings to congress and demonstrations and road blockades and responses to Environmental Impact Statements and meetings of Consensus groups...yet very little of a substantial nature has changed. Condors and jaguars and all sorts of amphibians and thousands of other species, all across the planet are on the way out. I'm sorry to sound negative; I hope your effort will make some new waves."

"Waves are good," Steve said. "I believe in waves. Ripples are nice too, but on the other hand there is such a thing as being too nice."

Jennifer, stepping carefully from the lab with ice cream, caught Steve's remark and announced that Breakout will not be too nice. "It will make waves, big ones. Batten the hatches."

Enid, startled, wondered where Jennifer had picked up such enthusiasm, such certitude? Why can't I be like that? Too old? Too tired? No. The loneliness syndrome, that was the bitter truth.

Later that afternoon Enid slowed to make the turn into her street in Rock River, but changed her mind and drove on to Medicine Bow. She kept on, crossed the river to open rangeland. She wanted a lift of heart, a sign. The sky had turned gray, covered by the bottoms of low clouds.

She parked and walked and came to a creek and sat on its turfy bank. The creek's slurpings and sloppings were very different from the high jangle of the creek at Sybille. The sounds ought to be soothing, but they weren't. She laid herself full length on the ground, looked up at the shades of gray. Why am I so deeply attached to this rashly contrived imaginary creature called Breakout? It's nothing more than a grouping around a heap of money. And look at the board of directors. Pitiful. A runaway wife; another runaway wife; two old crocks, one in a nursing home, the other surely headed that way. So, we're on the web, we've got a listserv. So's everybody else. Where's the fight? Where's the grit?

She sat up. "I could scream." And she did and the land soaked it up; nothing but faint echo, then utter silence came back to her, and as she stood, open-mouthed, listening, a few icy drops of rain touched her lips and her tongue. She noticed a distant cluster of ranch buildings sheltered by cottonwoods, illuminated by a shaft of sunlight. She stared hard at the brilliant glow on the ranch. It blinked out. A blast of wind ruffled the tips of sage and grass, bringing a heavy hammer of rain.

She took a shortcut to the car. In misty rain a sudden flurry, a scatter of many wings fixed in a long, low gliding pattern. Sage grouse. Enid counted them. Fourteen. "There," she said.

A subspecies of bighorns, total population down to something like 200 individuals, maybe less. Mountain lions take some of the lambs. Poachers look for trophy heads.

Last week three of us rambling in a canyon came upon five sheep, two ewes and three lambs, close up. They were in shade at the base of a high cliff, looking down at us. I'd known them only as mournful statistics, but on that day they were looking down at us very intently, very much alive and we guessed they were trying to figure out whether we were a danger. We were looking up at them, feeling ignorant. All of us, we talked about it later. I can't get that scene out of my mind. Desert sheep lived in these mountains thousands of years. I came here about three years ago, to get a new start in life. Can anybody tell me why I can't forget being near those sheep for a few minutes? Is it because I have been conditioned by TV? Have I been indoctrinated in some fuzzy nature love mindset? I'm really bothered by this idea of being a newcomer, a very restless newcomer, looking for a home. So many of us new to the land. Does that tell us something? Those sheep are at home. And they'll soon be gone.

Luke

Dear Jennifer,

Hanging out with Red. One day he introduced me to a law student named Lewis, a San Carlos Apache. Lewis doesn't want to do what a lot of other law degree Indians are doing, mainly court appeals against the government. He wants to be an organiser. "On the street," he says.

Red warned him, said he'd first have to use his skills to put food on the table. Lewis laughed, said survival went with being Indian.

Red argued with him on that too, his point being that there are good things beyond bare survival.

But Lewis's idea was that what you need is whatever you and your tribe or nation understands to be worth working for. Red wasn't quite happy with that either. He's one of these guys always looking for the disagreement side of what anybody says. He told Lewis there is danger in people stagnating by repeating the same rituals and customs, generation after generation. That's not living up to human creativity and potential.

Lewis sort of sighed and looked off across the street and said, "Nature won't let that happen."

Red jumped on that and he and Lewis went on hammering at each other, but I lost interest, stood there watching traffic for a while until Lewis asked us if we'd like to take a run down to the San Carlos Rez, have a look at the place the U. S. Cavalry picked out for rebel Apaches, a place no white people wanted.

Red and I both said, "Sure," but it ended up with just me and Lewis biking down there a couple days later, Lewis on a Yamaha and me on the hog. A long day of dirt and gravel roads and two-tracks and sometimes off-track. Saw a coyote and some hawks and a woodpecker on a saguaro and various birds in tamarisk and mesquite along the river. Also tracks of snakes and two different kinds of lizards. Hot as hell.

Near dark we got back to town, found a bar, ordered beer and sandwiches, talked about one thing and another. I mentioned Mount Graham, endangered squirrel country.

Lewis said, "Those animals deserve a life. It so happens the whole mountain deserves a life. Mount Graham is sacred to Apaches, my people. We have our own name for it. Wayne, can you tell me why so many people defending animals and habitats have a certain way of talking? Like, they throw in 'sacred mountain' like it was a tail-end piece of a big spiel. Like sacred to Apaches or Mohawks or Oglalas is just an extra item on a long list. You know what I'm saying?"

I wasn't sure I got what he was driving at.

He said, "Well, look, why can't you enviros make one great big buffalo bellow out of Indians' sacred places getting second-hand treatment? Like, you know, a mountain is just a natural feature, can't possibly come up to the real standard: Christian churches and Muslim mosques? Environmentalists, of all people, ought to pick up on this. But they don't. Look, squirrels and owls and bristlecone pines and tortoises and all the others deserve to live. Let's fight for them, that's cool, but what about places? Places on this earth are part of people's lives? What keeps people going? Does anybody wonder about that? Huh? You tell me."

I wanted to tell him I was just a garage worker from Montana. How the hell was I supposed to know what whites thought about this and that all over the country? But by then I knew he had more to say and I told him so.

"All right, amigo, one story. Mexican Spotted Owl, endangered species. Along comes the Bureau of Indian Affairs, pushing for logging timber on Indian land. All the usual good things: economic benefits, blah blah, standard line. They admit there is a down side, the destruction of spotted owl habitat, but that doesn't really pose a problem since 'the owl is held in low esteem' by Navaho and Apache people.' I'm giving you the exact quote, it's in a BIA document. We law students have to pay close attention to documents. 'Held in low esteem,' got it? Now, let's go to reality.

"Owls are part of a way of life, Indian lives, animal lives. People, anmals, places." He put his hands together to make a sort of hollow globe and looked hard at me and then down at his hands. He made little wiggles with his fingers and thumbs.

I said, "Things change."

"You got it, amigo. And humans try to make sense of it all. We use words. Here in what's left of Indian country our words tell us the owl is one of the dark creatures, a negative influence coming up against light and hope and human energy. The point is, without lights and darks and shadows you're not making sense, the story won't work."

I said, "You're not talking about environment, you're talking about nature, the whole shebang."

Lewis lit up with a big smile. "I am," he said. "All the stories."

I'm working on this. Hope all's well with you, and the ferrets..

Your friend, Wayne

To: BREAKOUT@LISTSERV.SPEAKUP.ORG

From: jkraus@texoco.com

Re: Houston Toad

Hi, I'm a grad student in economics at U. of Texas, Austin.

I spent two Saturdays in Bastrop State Park looking for a Houston toad, finally found one, /Bufo houstonensis/, about two inches long.

In 1978 the federal Fish and Wildlife Service put this species on the endangered list.

BTW fire ants eat young toads.

Andrea and I have decided to write a one-page info sheet (good heavy weight paper) about this animal and hand it out and keep handing it out. No pleas for money or mercy or action, just info, things people ought to know. Why are we doing this?

   Jason

To: BREAKOUT@LISTSERV.SPEAKUP.ORG

From: bweston@farwest.com

Re: Amphibians

Sad to say, another toad, /Bufo boreas/ is in trouble in the Colorado mountains. So far, biologists have found one cause of toad deaths, an exotic fungus that spreads its spores in water. But that's only one piece of the worldwide amphibian puzzle.

     Brian

To: BREAKOUT@LISTSERV.SPEAKUP.ORG

From: jkraus@texoco.com

Re: Amphibians

Brian, I agree, it is a huge puzzle. Not one simple cause but a snarl of causes. And I'm beginning to see how amphibians spell out not only their own crisis, but ours too.. Equally clear is domination by monster corporations turning every thing into market share. We ought to be looking at world economy and ecosystem intertwining.

     Jason

To: BREAKOUT@LISTSERV.SPEAKUP.ORG

From: lmacd@westelcom.com

Re: Corporations

Jason, I strongly disagree with your putting all the blame on "monster corporations." That's just empty rhetoric. We're all to blame, in the ways we choose to live, so extravagantly. To save species, and ourselves, we have to take all factors into account. Good luck with your toads. Here in Minnesota leopard frogs are in decline.

> Louise

To: BREAKOUT@LISTSERV.SPEAKUP.ORG

From: jkraus@texoco.com

Re: Corporations

Louise, As I see it, 'domination' by corporations is a fact. There are exceptions and plenty of complications in the corporate world, but the fact remains. I did not mean to imply that there are no other factors, including the blind extravagance in which so many of us choose to live. Want to hear more about your leopard frogs.

> Jason

Maple View.

Otis, crouched over the new computer, whispered, "Argument, good."

S̲ybille canyon.

Jennifer smiled. "Now we're truly launched."

R̲ock River.

"Oh my," Enid said, "all this wise talk. Is that all?"

T̲emecula, California

Dear Jennifer,

I said goodbye to Phoenix and headed south to Gila Bend where the old hog quit on me. Major overhaul. Second day of the overhaul job I cleaned up and went for lunch in the Cool Cat Cafe, picked up a newspaper somebody'd left on the counter, *High Country News*, read a piece about western willow flycatchers. They nest in brush on river banks of the Gila and a few other places, only a few hundred of them left. Usual story, habitats destroyed by cattle grazing and water projects. Later that day at auto parts I asked the guys there about the flycatcher. One of them told me he thought some bird out there on the Gila was in trouble, might be the one I was looking for.

I said I wasn't exactly looking for them, just curious. He suggested somebody who might know more, lives at the edge of town, a woman name of Lorraine McComb. He gave me directions. I guess she's the town's environmentalist. "Nice woman, wrong politics."

Next day the Hog was raring to go. I found this Lorraine McComb. She was sitting in an armchair in weak shade of a big old mesquite, reading a newspaper. She had long gray hair and wore granny glasses. The yard was packed dirt, no lawn.

She found another chair for me and we visited. Turned out she'd grown up in Powder River country, and now she's upset about the methane drilling going on up there. She subscribes to a couple of grassroots environment journals, but is beginning to think people don't really know what grassroots means.

I asked her what it means and she hesitated a while, then warned me that all she was going on were her own fuzzy, private thoughts and I said that's all I went on too.

She said, "All right, I'll try, and then I'll go make us some ice tea. I imagine grassroots as millions of people everywhere, keeping the planet limping along. Nurses and tractor repair people, hardware clerks and checkout workers and warehouse workers and truck drivers, plumbers and electricians and trouble shooters of all kinds. People. Nameless people. Think of people, Wayne. They're working the fields and the sweatshops and assembly lines. Doing things. Coming up against problems and some of those problems are horrific, but some are nicely solved by human cleverness. We are a very clever species. It's those millions and millions of people who keep things going. It's not smart talk doing that job, not just reams of print on paper. It's laughing and dancing and getting along and not getting along. It's death and destruction. All those things.

"Well, from time to time, somehow or other, a sort of slow simmer begins, there in the deeps, where the roots are. New things show up. It does happen, it has happened. I dare to believe that this is one of those times."

I said I could agree with the simmering part.

She smiled, but then she tossed her head like a balky horse, as if she was mad, said, "Level with me, Wayne."

So, you see, it was my turn. That talking we all did in Medicine Bow, the four of us, and Otis on the phone, and the Mount Graham red squirrel arguments in Phoenix and talking to Lewis in San Carlos and long hours on the road, just me and the hog, well, you can imagine I had quite a lot to tell Lorraine. Won't bore you with it, except to say I ended up with how I thought the simmering had to be red hot to amount to anything truly new.

Lorraine laughed. She said, "Of course."

She invited me into her house and made the tea and I learned some things about willow flycatchers. Naturally we got into other species too. We were in the kitchen, leaning on the counter, sipping the tea, Lorraine looking out the window. A stray thought drifted into my mind and I said it. "Maybe all the species are in the grass, the roots."

Lorraine frowed. I felt foolish, but then she said, "Yes, they'd have to be, wouldn't they? Otherwise we are still outside looking in"

Ought to write to her. Lewis too. But first, this to you, which is way too long, but I have to add one more thought that showed up three or four days later (I lose track of time) in California north of San Diego when I turned off the highway looking for a camp site, traveled a mile or two into low hills covered with grass waving in a light wind and evening sun shimmering on ripe leaves and heads of grass, sending patches of light into shadowed parts of the hills. I grew up in rangeland in Montana, thought I knew about grass, but until then I'd never thought of grass doing work. Work of the world, that's what they're up to, the many different kinds.

These are lonesome roads.

Your friend,

Wayne

Rufus found a cafe in Farson, listened to a pair of ranchers discuss local affairs. Intricate, tantalising, but there were too many loose ends for a visitor from the far east. He drove on, many a mile, high skies and expansive plains turning dark. On the east side of Rock Springs he found a small, low-price motel. In the morning, admitting he'd had enough of west wandering, he took I-80 east.

At Buford he bought gas, a Leanin' Tree postcard, a Mountain Dew, a turkey sandwich, and asked if there was any way to cross Nebraska other than I-80.

The proprietor was happy to oblige. "Stay on I-80 to I-25, then north to U.S. 20 and you're home free. Good road all the way. I'd suggest you stop off at Museum of the Fur Trade, just the other side of Chadron."

"Fur trade?"

"Just trust me on that. You only live once, isn't that right?"

"That is the truth," Rufus said.

He went north...Chugwater, Wheatland, McKinley...turned east on 20. At Chadron, Nebraska, a grand flame of sunset behind him, he found a motel, surfed across a blur of insult, zapped it off, flopped back on the bed, slept well. He got under way late in the morning, barely settled into travel rhythm when the Museum of the Fur Trade showed up. Easy access, good parking. He stopped.

Long hallways, exhibits on both sides. Beaver traps; bear traps; long rifles of unbelievable heft and length; sealskins; sea otter skins; buffalo hides and buffalo robes; trade goods: beads, copper wire, hatchets, tomahawks, rifles, bullets, lead, bullet molds, flints, powder, tobacco in big braided ropes, tobacco as bricks...all of them real objects in history, a few hundred years on the place we call North America. The Spanish, the French, the Russians, the English, the Swedes and the Dutch; the Indian nations and the Inuit and the Aleuts.

He came to the end of the hall, another hall branched from there. An hour had passed. He returned to the entrance, made a wrong turning, found himself outside on a narrow path that led to two log dugouts. He consulted the four-page handout that had been given to him along with his admission ticket. He was standing on the site of the Bordeaux Trading Post, established in 1837 by the American Fur Company. Downhill and to his left was the log dugout identified as the Trade Room. Its logs were fitted together by dovetail notches and the roof was dirt over poles, growing a crop of mature, yellowed cheat grass.

It seemed that all of Nebraska had suddenly shut down in total silence under a high cloudless sky, in gentle heat of morning. Rufus studied the dovetails of the gray, brittle and finely fissured log ends of the Trade Room. He leaned back against the warm front of the building, closed his eyes, heard only one sound, small bird scratching in dry leaves.

Footsteps and a voice. "Are you all right?"

He lurched out from the wall, looked uphill. A woman stood there, tall and erect, dark brown eyes and black bangs streaked with white in the shade of a straw hat.

"I'm fine," Rufus said.

"Beautiful morning."

"Yes."

She came down the path, stepping neatly. "I know this place, know it well," she said as she came up to him and stood very close and looked at him with no apology. "I come here often."

"My first time."

"You will return."

He looked at her, studied her. He wasn't embarrassed. Her own outgoing manner seemed to invite scrutiny.

She smiled. "No, I'm not a shill, just an admirer of this place. A person can be quiet here and imagine Oglala and Brule Sioux on that hillside over there. In winter when the hunting is not so urgent, they bring buffalo hides. Thousands of horses, hundreds of lodges."

Rufus said, "I'm from the east, never thought much about any of this."

"None of us do, really, think about these things. Sometimes I meditate, usually in the entrance, right there where you're standing. Sometimes up there at the buffalo hide press."

Rufus looked uphill, noticed a long, heavy log, one end propped between uprights.

"That's the press," the woman said. The Indian women tanned the hides, you know. Think of the labor of that. Just think of it. Don't let your mind wander away from that, the tanning, the hand work, prolonged, urgent. The men traded five robes for a rifle, three robes for a blanket."

"You'd think a robe would be better than a blanket."

"The blankets were wool, of course. You might have noticed the Hudson Bay blankets inside? High quality, I assume. I hope so. Perhaps blankets were lighter than buffalo skins, easier to pack on horses. There is so much we don't know with real certainty. My name is Maureen."

"Rufus. Math teacher, retired, never got into history much."

"I manage Joseph's Restaurant in Chadron and write for the Chadron newspaper."

He smiled. "And you're writing a novel."

"Does it show that much? All right, you nailed me. I was working on a novel, about James Bordeaux's two Indian wives. They were sisters, daughters of a Brule chief. I wanted so much to enter into their ways of feeling about men and marriage and children and life in these wilds, but there was no entering their lives, for me. You see, it all happened so fast, the conquest of the plains, from the Sioux rebellion at the time of our Civil War to Little Big Horn and the death of Crazy Horse. All over in a few decades, so few testimonies. What brings you here, Rufus?"

He was stumped. Beyond admitting that he was on the margins of society, what was there to say? He wasn't about to reveal that his life didn't amount to much more than sipping coffee in McDonald's, reading newspapers, waiting for spring and the warbler migration. But a saving thought came. "I'm in the endangered species business."

Maureen clapped her hands. "Oh good, I've been brooding over that. Very near hopeless, isn't it?"

"We'll find out. We're just getting started. We have some money and a name."

"What's the name?"

"Breakout."

She broke into rambunctious laughter. "Oh that's grand, and I hope it means what it says. You know what that name says, don't you? It says you're going to walk the talk. If you don't, I'm no longer your friend."

"Yup, we'll be walking." He surprised himself by giving her a flirtatious sidewise glance. "Wouldn't want to lose your friendship."

"Good. Now listen, Rufus, I'm your Nebraska critic. Don't let me down, and next time you're in Chadron, come to Joseph's. It's upscale. Yes, we do have one of those, you better believe it."

To: BREAKOUT@LISTSERV.SPEAKUP.ORG
From: sandys@hotmail.com
Re: Copperbelly snake

I live in Indiana where the copperbelly is uncommon. Further north in Michigan it's even scarcer.

Two years ago, just out of high school, a couple of us fooling around in some bottomlands, never mind where, that has to be a secret (remember, this snake is at risk, or endangered, I forget which). My friend lets out a humongous scream and turns around so fast he falls down and he's crawling on the ground not getting anywhere he's so shook up. He'd come across a copperbelly, a big one. It gave me a shock too, but I'm one of those freaks who likes snakes, maybe because once when I was a kid a gartersnake hypnotized me. I'm not kidding. In the garden, weeding, bored to death, stopped weeding, sat there feeling sorry and I see this flickering motion, a snake's shiny tongue. Gartersnake, had its chin resting on a dry stem of a last year's tomato plant. I stared and stared at that tongue tasting the air. And the eye, staring without a blink. That started me on snakes.

Copperbelly's other name: /Nerodia erythrogaster neglecta/.

Sandy

V alentine, Nebraska.

Rufus arrived long after sundown, found a motel and called Otis.

"Rufus, where the hell have you been?"

"Here and there, doesn't matter."

"Wrong. It does matter. Jennifer and Enid keep calling me up at ten o'clock Eastern Daylight. That's bedtime here in this gulag."

"Why can't a man go off on a little traveling without people getting all possessive?"

Otis calmed down. "Possessive, uh huh, I know what you mean. So, what's up with you?"

"I'm in Valentine."

"I'm supposed to know where that is?"

"Nebraska. I'm headed east, I guess. Hard to tell. You about ready for that cruise to Costa Rica?"

"Forget Costa Rica. Quit harping on it."

"We've saved up for it, Otis. What's got into you?"

"We have more important things on the agenda just now."

"Agenda? That sounds scary. What are you talking about?"

"Breakout."

Otis's voice had changed. Rufus knew his friend too well to miss it. The old crock was excited, trying to hide it.

"Listen, old man," Otis continued, "listen good. I don't know what trouble you're in, wandering all over the country, but I'm glad you called. The news is that we are into Breakout, in deep; for better or worse, that's where we are."

Silence, Rufus taking it in. He said. "I'm all for Breakout. Who was it flew clear out to Medicine Bow to confer with Enid and Jennifer? Me, that's who. But I don't see why we can't slip in a week or so in the cloud forests."

"Sure, but I'm not in the mood right now, that's the honest truth. Tagging along behind ever-so-polite and condescending bird guides in some tropical paradise, I don't know, seems sort of silly right now. Sorry."

"I'll call you later." Rufus hung up.

To: BREAKOUT@LISTSERV.SPEAKUP.ORG

From: annbr@wyoming.com

Subject: Zapus

I saw a jumping mouse! I held it on my hand! We caught it in a live trap. The BLM guy who did all the expertise put the trap in a bag and closed the bag around his left arm. Then he pushed on the bag to open the trap and the mouse scrambled into the bag and the guy grabbed where the mouse was and then he took the mouse by the tail, near the base. He cautioned me about that. If you get your hold out near the tip of the tail it just breaks and goodbye mouse. So, he hauled it out and put it on the back of his left hand.

Zapus is different from any mouse I've ever seen. Its tail is unbelievably long. It's not like mice we're used to. Its fur has a mixture of brown and yellow with black hairs mixed in so it has a kind of peppery look.

I got a good hold on its tail and lifted it onto my hand. That took some nerve. It didn't bite, just sat there, but its body was tense, I could feel it. The belly fur is pure white. I let go the tail and wow, that mouse made a huge jump into the grass and then another jump must have been at least a foot and a half high, and then gone and you'd never even think there might be a little mouse living there.

I've learned they hibernate for a long time. Also, they do like to be near water, so that means the ranchers have a problem trying to avoid killing them along creeks and irrigation ditches.

All these Zapus species habitats go down into Colorado and north into Canada, originally, but most of their places are gone now. Cities, crops, suburbs. Cubin, our rep. in congress, is wrong. It does live in Wyoming. I know, I held one on my hand.

Anna

Driving out of Valentine, Rufus turned onto U.S. 83, trundled north, vaguely aware that the sun was in the wrong place. He passed a sign welcoming him to South Dakota, kept going, not knowing why. At a junction he stopped, to think. No vehicle passed by, nobody rode his tail. Sounds of grasshoppers drifted in from the vast land and a quietness settled into Rufus's very bones, his body-mind in charge, cut loose, on its own, or so it seemed, He raised his hands from the wheel, let them fall to a fresh grip and drove on, north. "Makes no sense," he said.

To: BREAKOUT@LISTSERV.SPEAKUP.ORG
From: dlamb@aol.com
Re: Flower-loving Fly

No ordinary fly, its full name is Delhi Sands Flower-loving fly. About an inch long, feeds on nectar of only a few plant species. They live now in just two California counties: San Bernardino and Riverside. Urban sprawl, etc. is one huge problem. My hope that this obscure fly will survive is all mixed up with my wish for cities to be real cities, not great octopi expanding forever.

Don

Maple View, New York.

Otis had a visitor, well muscled though severely stooped "I'm Paul Gallegos from Harbor View."

"Harbor View?"

"You know, sister to Maple View."

"Didn't know we had a sister."

"We're a chain and they're all *views*. One over in Connecticut is Ocean View. There's a High Sky View somewhere west of here."

Gallegos eased himself onto a chair. "I've come about Breakout."

Otis was surprised. "Breakout's barely off the ground. How did you find us so fast?"

Gallegos shifted on the uncomfortable chair, using his cane as a lever. "We found your website. That's three or four of us walking wounded still taking an interest in what goes on. One of us got on your listserv, posted a note on a rare bird in the Adirondacks."

"I remember that one," Otis said. "Bicknell's thrush. High mercury levels in blood and feathers. I posted a brief reply."

"Right. That's how we tracked you down. The thrush guy, Sam, he's competent, not just blowing smoke. Academic background, radical." Gallegos leaned forward. "I've travelled clear up here and believe me it wasn't easy, to ask if you have any idea what computers mean to us warehoused folks?"

Otis nodded. "I do."

"Oh, I'll grant you," Gallegos went on, "you can say, and you'd be mostly right, getting into Breakout is just a way to pass time. Hell yes, I say, there's that aspect to it. Time drags, you know."

Otis murmured, "Tell me about it."

Gallegos held up an arthritic hand. "I'm not saying the *years* don't fly away like snowflakes in July; it's these *days* and these goddamn *hours*. Well, I'm not planning on too many more years. No, not this body."

Otis said, "I'm counting on Avian Flu, West Nile, something like that."

"Yes, those are good. Quick outs. My Breakout research, incidentally, will concern fish in the Hudson river, methyl mercury muck in the bottom, polluted tributaries, the whole situation.

I'll tie in with Pete Seeger's outfit. You know about River Keepers?"

"Yes."

"Let me introduce myself. In my former life I had a small business over in Newark, so I have a business man's view of things, but also a concern for nature, the way we're trashing the planet. And now I'm about to twist your arm and beg a favor. At Harbor View one computer is not enough. It's in a little room next to the Assisted Living wing, where Sam and Helen and I stay, but the whole damned HMO has access to it. You can imagine the long waits for access, and once you get on you've barely got started when you have to get off. And the squabbles we get into, you wouldn't believe."

"No, I believe. Is it a Mac?"

"Right. And that's what you've got."

"How come you know so much about us?"

"You suppose there's an underground network hooking up nursing homes?" He laughed. "You know, that's probably the god's truth. So, Otis...can I call you Otis?...these squabbles at Harbor View are driving us bats. There's three of us...me, Sam and Helen... ready to go whole hog with Breakout. We desperately need on-line time. Three musketeers at your service. Let me repeat this, Otis: we're into Break-out for the long haul."

Otis, a veteran of the sixties and early seventies, its dreams and actual victories, and along the way a disdain for power trips, felt in himself a little trip surge that worried him as he prepared to heave himself up from his chair. "All right, Paul, let's go look at the Breakout computer. Then we'll talk about your problem. Maybe I can fix you up."

To: BREAKOUT@LISTSERV.SPEAKUP.ORG

From: ewilson@earthlink.com

Re: Flower-loving Fly

I'm a veteran watcher of development pressures in Salt Lake City metro area. That's why I have to tell everybody on this list that the flower-loving fly in California is doomed. It's best and largest refuge, a few hundred acres of unique sandy ecosystem, is almost entirely owned by a sand and gravel company. AND, it is included in California's Agua Mansa Enterprise Zone. Can those "development" tides be held back? No, not a chance, unless something really different happens in time, in California, in the nation.

What might a really different happening be? I don't know. There might be a very slight chance if a charismatic mammal lived there, something more lovable than kangaroo rats. But who gives a damn about an inch-long fly?

Reality folks, we have to face it, and cry.

Echo

Sylvie Rhodes came to the social room early, as was her custom. She brought toast and coffee to her usual table, on the line where blue linoleum changed to yellow brown, the boundary between social and kitchen spaces. She eased herself onto a metal chair and sat still for a few moments, catching her breath. A cancer surviver, Sylvie currently suffered nothing but aches and pains and the relentless boredom of age. She would turn 75 next week. No one visited her or called her. She didn't moan about it, the way Babs Blaine did, wanting the whole world to know. But Babs could be jolly too. She was Sylvie's one friend at Maple View, self-centered as all-get-out, for which Sylvie was grateful. She felt safe with Babs. There she was now, moving awkwardly to the kitchen's serving counter. She would join Sylvie. They would breakfast together, then Sylvie would go to the Breakout computer. It was a new lease on life, that computer. They loved it, the big bright screen, the colored icons inviting them to anywhere and everywhere, the fantastic speed, new views, more invites. And Breakout was a good place to visit along the way, though its talk was seldom uplifting.

Sylvie had decided to learn about whales, especially the blue whale, a remote seldom-seen mammal. Somewhere in the vast world of oceans the males and females met and mated, but we humans didn't know where. And it was huge, largest living animal, ever.

On this fine July day Sylvie planned to add to what she had posted earlier, a few carefully chosen sentences from the famous Moby Dick chapter on the architecture of the whale. She had been a little bothered by that post, wondering if it had been too bookish alongside the other threads thus far on Breakout that told of direct experience and personal confession. But she had decided that there was nothing wrong with trying to imagine other lives, by whatever means lay at hand.

She watched Herb Swanson walk to the counter. Herb's age was about the same as hers. She envied his loose-jointed walk that carried his weight well. His only serious defect, Sylvie happened to know, was a dicey circulatory system. Sylvie smiled, noticing the way Herb scanned the room as though he owned it. Suddenly, he froze in place, his breakfast tray clanged on the counter, his mouth opened, no sound emerged. Sylvie thought, "Oh dear, his heart," But no, he was taking big strides to the new computer. It wasn't there.

Herb shouted, "What the fuck?"

The old Quadra squatted in its usual place, against the windowless wall. On its right, where the Breakout computer had been, nothing. Sylvie's outside world, a world without walls, world of mystery, all gone in that sudden explosion from Herb, "What the fuck?" The words rang in Sylvie's ears and she was repeating them softly. "What the fuck?"

To: BREAKOUT@LISTSERV.SPEAKUP.ORG

From: mokada@aol.com

Re: Suisun thistle

I live in San Francisco, but know the marsh habitat of the endangered suisun thistle. There are other species there, including some "officially" rated threatened or endangered. Anong these are ornate shrews, suisun song sparrow, suisun aster and clapper rail. Many visitors too, including hawks and peregrine falcons.

These tidal marshes are SYSTEMS. Trying to save one species at a time leaves way too much room for cutting incredibly complicated habitats into little patches. Plants and animals need space and variability, they need refuges, places to recover from disaster or years/seasons unfavorable. We humans need that too, very badly. Not just wilderness, but prime land for growing food and surviving climate change, war damage, stupid development projects.

Marie

Maple View, New York.

They fumed and fussed for a day and a night and then came together on Maple View's patio, gathering there not by appointment but by common distress.

Otis and Herb and Maud had been casual acquaintances, but Otis had only a barebones recognition of Babs. He and Herb knew Sylvie only in her role as clever fixer of computer sulks. Maud and Herb sometimes gossiped together. Sylvie was very tight with Babs, otherwise kept aloof.

"Printout of people posting on Breakout," Otis said, slapping down three pages of hardcopy on the metal table that was still damp from rain, but now the sun was out in a sky decorated with high cirrus.

"Where'd you get that?" Herb asked. He grabbed the sheets, scanned, looking for his own name. There it was, with the title of his contribution, Whitebark Pine. He'd happened upon a news item in USA Today; scientists in some Forest Service lab had developed a strain of whitebark pine relatively resistant to white pine blister rust, whatever that was. Herb's interest in endangered species was of very recent origin, dating from the day the Breakout computer arrived.

Otis said, "I had it sent from Rock River, Breakout headquarters."

"Where's that?" Babs asked, her voice clear, melodious, penetrating, a blessing for Otis's and Herb's impaired hearing.

"Small town, in Wyoming."

"Cheaper that way," Herb said.

Otis said, "Yes, but mainly it just happened. Jennifer works in the black-footed ferret lab, up a canyon not too far from Rock River, so she and Enid get together without too much trouble."

"Two women?" Sylvie asked. "Is that all Breakout is?"

"It's all of us."

"Which is all nice and cozy," Herb said, "but it's time you leveled with us, Otis. Who really does the heavy lifting out there in the wilds of Wyoming?"

"You're too secretive, Otis," Babs said.

Otis reared back, stared at her. "That's utterly ridiculous. How did you ever get that idea?"

"Oh, hard to explain. Little details, like what kind of people are they, those two women? What's their ages, where do they come from, their families, what they wear, who do they go around with."

"Jesus," Otis breathed. "I don't know what they wear; have never laid eyes on those women. I know them through Rufus and on the phone."

Herb broke in. "Never mind all that. Beside the point. What do we do about that Breakout computer?"

"Herb, you're as bad as Otis," Maud said. "Keep your cards so close to your chest you can't even read them yourself. We all know you and Otis yesterday had a run-in with Maple View's manager. Both of you guys owe us. Give, the whole story."

"Treated us like seniles," Herb said. "Then Otis here, he starts in about rights and all that, which gives that smooth-faced weasel a chance to get off the subject."

"No," Otis said, " it gave him a chance to fall back on the Patriot Act. Threat to national security. He exposed himself."

The three women were stunned. They looked at each other. Babs said, "You got to be kidding."

"It's true," Herb conceded, "he did harp on *National Security*. But first he fobbed us off with some hogwash about not accepting gifts from unknown donors, least of all donors who had axes to grind. I jumped him on that, mentioned that the old Mac was a donation too, anonymous. Then Otis sounded off again, about patients' rights. I glazed over, so did...what's the manager's name?"

"Last name's something like Wiken," Sylvie said. "So then he told you Breakout might be a terrorist penetration."

Otis and Herb turned sharply, looked at Sylvie as if they'd never seen her before. "Good Lord," Herb said, and Otis, desperately trying to recall her name, said, "You must have been a fly on the wall." Like a blessing from on high, her name came. "Sylvie," he said, "you nailed it, dead center. *Terrrorist penetration*, those were his very words."

She smiled at her clasped hands. "Lots of people use those words." She looked up at Otis. "What else did he say?"

Otis and Herb spoke at once, outraged at the treatment they'd received, the gist of which was that Maple View had been cautioned by its

Pittsburgh management honchos to be vigilant, to notice any development that was in any way out of the ordinary, a break with the usual routines.

"You guys ought to have told us," Maud said. "You should have talked to Babs and Sylvie and me and then we could have all gone together to brace this Wikens weasel."

"Yes," Babs said, "and then we could have had a real blow-up."

"And what would that have accomplished?" Otis asked.

"I don't know," Babs replied, unruffled. "We would have been in it all together is what I'm saying."

Otis sighed that condescending sigh that all of them noticed and disliked. They waited for the pronouncement that always followed, but this time it didn't come.

Herb said, "Otis, that leftwing professor stuff you kept throwing at him, gave him a chance to put you down hard, put me down too. You stiffened the guy's spine. Didn't you see that?"

Sylvie giggled, Maud smiled, Babs' eyes twinkled, and Otis turned slowly, deliberately to face Herb with the blankest stare he could muster. "Patient's rights, freedom of speech, call them leftwing all you want, but somebody had to stick up for them. And by the way, you've got me pegged wrong. In my former life I was a businessman."

"Not a professor?"

"No way a professor."

"What kind of business?"

"Veterinarian."

" I ran a laundromat. Twenty nine years."

"I didn't know that."

"Well now you know."

"And now we all know," Babs said, and Maud said, "For god sake, you guys." Her gaunt cheeks framed a derisive grin. "Enough of the entertainment."

Sylvie said, "What happens to us now?"

Silence, and for the first time all five of them noticed listeners, fellow residents only a few steps away, in wheelchairs and on cushioned benches soaking up sunshine at the edge of the patio.

"Actually," Maud said, "robbery by management is a crime."

"Sure," Herb said, "but spouting off about it isn't always a good idea."

Otis sighed again. "Maybe you're right."

Babs, short and heavy, sat up straight and took on an air of dignity. "There *is* such a thing as free speech, and the internet is a place we all can really do it, let down our hair. It's where everybody gets to say whatever they want, like a big town meeting. I know about those, being from Vermont, except on the internet nobody gets to hog all the time. You just push some big self-important blabbermouth into the trash. Poof, he's gone."

Otis began to speak, thought better of it.

Maud said, "I applaud those sentiments and agree all the way, but here in Maple View, right now, today, our computer is gone and we' can't do a damn thing about it and I am totally pissed off and by god I feel like getting up and walking out of here and never coming back. I think I'd like to die, out there."

"Me too," Sylvie said.

To: BREAKOUT@LISTSERV.SPEAKUP.ORG

From: csant@earthlink.com

Re: Wyoming Toad

Jason, your toad isn't the only one at risk. In 1994 Wyoming's /Bufo baxteri/ was declared 'extinct in the wild.' There is a population in captivity, but when some of these are released in natural habitats they don't do well.

Species so restricted, even before humans came along, why bother trying to bring them back? And that jumping mouse,

Zapus hudsonius preblei, is only a "sub" species, and now some biologists think it isn't even a subspecies. Would the ecosystem fall apart if it went extinct? Just wondering.

Cerise

To: BREAKOUT@LISTSERV.SPEAKUP.ORG

From: jkraus@texoco.com

Re: Wyoming Toad

Cerise, I don't know the answer. My toad, nearing extinction in one little state park in Texas, might not matter a whit. But before that toad completely disappears, I want people to know about it.

Jason

To: BREAKOUT@LISTSERV.SPEAKUP.ORG

From:: annbr@wyoming.com

Re: Wyoming toad

No! I don't care whether Wyoming Zapus is a susbspecies or not; the BLM biologist tells me the Endangered Species Act says the 'historic range' of a species is to be saved, as far as possible.

Even if it didn't say that, I would say it. I don't see any reason why Zapus can't be allowed to live here. Excuse me, but who the hell owns Wyoming, anyway? Out of state oil and gas and trona and coal companies? If you could only SEE a Zapus!!

Anna

Rufus browsed in a huge box store, in Pierre, South Dakota. Sporting goods and outdoor adventure opportunities, from extra-long leverage nail clippers to chartered polar bear hunts. He stopped at the book and magazine section, noticed *Hawks*, by Clark and Wheeler. He bought it and went back to the car and leaned against it in the dry heat, vaguely contemplating directions. North, south, east, west. He chose east, ended the day at a Super 8 in Sioux Falls. At the cooler ending of the next day he found a modest motel in a town just west of Duluth and called Otis.

Otis asked, "What's got into you?"

Rufus said, wearily. "Wish I knew. Sorry I hung up on you."

"Where are you?"

"Near Duluth." He was looking into the motel parking lot where an erratic wind twirled dust, papers, plastics. A pizza carton cartwheelied into view. An errant gust lifted it high, it spread its wing and soared until the wind slammed it onto the hood of a four-door Toyota. It scooted across the shiny surfce only to be slammed again. Rufus lost sight of it. He said, "We're not in charge. Nobody is."

"I know," Otis said. "I thought we decided that, long time ago."

"We did. I've been traveling, decided it all over again."

"All right. I suspect you're suffering from late life crisis. It's worse where I am. Now, let's see, you're at west end of Lake Superior. You'll go east from there. Hmmm, northern Michigan, above the mitten. How'm I doing?"

"Sounds right."

"Assuming you don't cross into Canada, you come south into Michigan's mitten and...hey, Kirtland's."

"Warblers?"

"I think so. Hang on, I'll get Peterson."

Sounds of Otis breathing, pages turning. "Here we are. Habitat second growth jack pine, ground cover of blueberries, bearberry or sweet fern."

"Range?"

"North central Michigan, nesting in loose colonies in an area about 100 miles long, 60 miles wide. Winters in the Bahamas."

Silence, thoughts of Kirtland's warblers. Rufus said, "Good, something to do. I'll hole up down there somewhere, stay a day or two. Truth is, I don't want to go home."

"You're lucky to have a house to call your own, to be boss of."

"Not a house, it's an apartment. Thanks for the warbler tip."

To: BREAKOUT@LISTSERV.SPEAKUP.ORG

From: mtorres@newportnet.net

Re: Subspecies

Getting back to the subspecies question. I say, if we compromise here we lose essential ground. We are forced to be flexible on a lot of things, but on certain principles a firm line has to be drawn. The Endangered Species Act says that the "historic range" of a species has to be restored "in so far as possible." That's flexy enough. If ranges happen to comprise a few sub-species, so be it, rescue them, be generous. Can we afford it? Yes, we can. It's just a matter of deciding. Politicians are like twelve-year olds, they have to be told, and told again and again, what to do and, especially, what not to do.

matt

Kingston, New York.

Otis and Enid in conference in Enid's rental, a block south of Maple View.

Otis said, "You didn't have to fly clear back here to talk to me."

"On the contrary, it *was* necessary. It's important to talk to you, in person. Phone conversation and e-mail go only so far. Now, we've both got problems and my plane leaves in two hours. My most immediate problem is this New Jersey group. Their new Breakout computer was also taken away and Paul what's-his-name has e-mailed me about it. I don't know quite how to reply to him."

"Paul's been onto me too. He's the kind of guy thinks if you talk to enough people in charge of things, something will be done. What's really weird about all this is that Paul and his two colleagues are taking the same crazy line that my people at Maple View are on."

"Which is?"

"Worked themselves up to where they're ready to walk out."

"Transfer to another home?"

"No. Like a suicide pact, walk the streets and highways till they drop. I think they really mean it."

"Tell me more, about your fellow...sorry, I don't know how to refer to them."

"Inmates. That's the preferred term, among us."

"Among you folks, yes, but I can't use it."

Otis chuckled. "The current approved term is *residents*."

"All right. Tell me about them."

"Well, let's see. Sylvie is into whales. I think she has an honest fascination there. Herb posted some boilerplate about whitebark pine; his appreciation of species is pretty much confined to being thankful for the new computer. As for Maud, she's from the midwest somewhere; Kansas maybe; talks about grassland, original prairie; I think that's sincere. She posted a quote from Wes Jackson. You know him? Co-founder of the Land Institute?"

"Otis, I'm a raw learner in these environmental fields. And there's aother woman, isn't there, in your group?"

"Babs, from Vermont; I haven't the faintest idea what she thinks about ecological matters. Maybe nothing."

"And you, Otis?"

"Birdwatcher, as you know."

"And what is your take on these threats to walk out?"

"If they walk out, I go with them."

Enid thought about it. "What should we do?"

"I was thinking we could make a trade. Us old crocks might contribute some minimal actions, out on the road, or some place outside the HMO system. Something simple to start with, maybe like what those people down in Houston are doing."

"Oh yes, Jason and Andrea and their friends. Houston toad people."

"As a beginning. We could discover bolder moves later." He waited now, hunched over in the passenger seat, waited for Enid to fall back onto that death-dealing word: *incompetence*. Stiff and stubborn, his body clenched into immobility as swarms of condescensions and dismissals from out of the Golden Years swarmed in his mind. Like deer flies, real biters. He was damned if he'd be the one to let them loose. That would be Enid's job, and then that would be that. But he heard her say, "What kind of help might Breakout provide?"

He said, "A bus."

To: BREAKOUT@LISTSERV.SPEAKUP.ORG

From: calbock@frontiernet.net

Re: Flower loving fly

Heard a lawyer for developers complain on NPR today, that half of California's privately owned land is classified by Fish and Wildlife as critical habitat for endangered species.

Anything wrong with that? I'm surprised the feds had the guts to come right out and say that hundreds of other species might have some claim to as much as half of what this one species, H. sapiens, thinks it owns.

I agree with Echo, something REALLY different has to happen. Cal

Enid re-scheduled her return flight to Wyoming, drove north to Albany and checked into a motel. She scanned the phone book's yellow pages, found Adventure Tours. An hour and a half later she walked into the spacious corner office of the assistant manager of Adventure Tours. She was graciously received.

He was a youngish man glowing with enthusiasm. "Eco-Tourism," he said, with a wave of his hand. "The wave of the future."

"My organization's goal is authenticity," Enid said. "We strive for active interaction with nature, a hands-on approach, not mere passivity."

"I know exactly what you mean. It's a worthy goal. I think our country is forging a new relationship with nature."

"I do hope so," she said. "When in the field we insist on active participation. We aim to place our clients in positions to make decisions. There is so much that ordinary people can do to preserve wilderness or enhance the opportunities for others …" Good lord, she thought, I'm really good at this.

The Assisstant Manager beamed, then got down to hands-on paper work, a document in triplicate. But Enid waved that aside. "I'm afraid I'll have to insist on interviewing the driver of the bus. That's so important, I'm sure you understand."

"Oh absolutely, and I think I have just the man for you. Suppose I refer you to our fleet superintendant. Meanwhile, I'll have the papers drawn up."

Enid found herself in the clang and motor roar of a huge garage, talking first to the superintendant, then to a cheerful young driver. His hands were nicotine stained. Enid apologized. "I ought to have been more specific. I'm afraid it has to be a strictly non-smoking environment."

"We don't smoke inside the bus."

"Yes, I assumed that to be the case, but we're trying to create an environment...oh, it's hard to explain." Enid had no idea whether Maud or Herb or Babs or Sylvie might be a chain smoker, or whether one of them might be trying to quit. But that was a secondary consideration because she had a gut feeling that this driver was not right for the Breakout bus.

The driver took it well, reached into his jacket for a smoke, flashed a wide grin and turned to shout into the racket of the garage. "She wants a non-smoker."

Enid said, "I'm sorry."

"No problem. Hey, I'll go rustle you up somebody."

Enid waited. She studied the bus behemoths, realizing that she hadn't paid much attention to buses in her life of upscale travel. Shouts echoed in the garage. Another driver appeared, a dark-haired man, less than average height and with a pencil thin mustache above a smile, but there was an alert skepticism in his middle-age eyes. "I'm Leonard," he said.

"I'm Enid Shaw, looking for a driver who wouldn't mind doing something a little different."

He raised an eyebrow, kept silent, waited. She liked that. "Something that has a mission attached."

"A mission," he said. "That would be interesting."

She threw caution to the winds. "Leonard, may I tell you the whole story?"

To: BREAKOUT@LISTSERV.SPEAKUP.ORG

From: hsand@mac.com

Re: corporations.

Sure, monster corporations dominate, but our attitudes back them. Remember the wolf incident in Montana, a pack of wolves made the mistake of killing a family dog? Murder! The feds got in a chopper, gunned down almost the whole pack.

Family dogs killed night and day on highways. We take that as normal tragedy for each family to endure. But a wolf kill is different: the perps have to be punished. Death penalty.

Hiram

Grayling, Michigan.

Rufus called Otis, reported on Kirtland's warblers. "No success yet, but a guy retired from Michigan Fish and Game gave me a map with a couple likely spots. Meanwhile visited with a crested flycatcher. Weather's good. There's a big National Guard post here, but I don't care; the whole country's militarizxed to the hilt anyway. I'm staying at a low price motel at the edge of town."

"What town?"

"Grayling."

"Low price motel."

"Yup. The owner's a Scandihoovian, originally from Fargo. Wife died just last year. Even in July and August he sometimes doesn't get all his units taken. He's about to fold."

"How many units?"

"Hey, why the quiz?"

"There've been a few developments."

"I see. You're into something."

"Afraid so. Something stupid, could use some help."

"Sure."

"Tell me a little more about the motel. We might need it."

"Tell me what's going on."

Otis hesitated. "It's pretty wild."

"I'm in the mood for that."

"Five of us barely-on-our-feet crocks are getting out of here. Enid hired a bus for us, and a driver."

"Breakout money."

"Yes, and don't tell me it's a waste of money. We're determined, that ought to count for something. Tell me what you really think."

"I think in a bus you can travel, work for species."

"How?"

"You tell me."

"No."

Suddenly, a vision, the airport at Casper, Wyoming, the change of plan and all the changes since piled helter skelter against the motel's blank wall. Buttes, mountains, great spreads of sage and grass; violet-green swallows at the great rock; dead animals on the highways; early morning light on orange antelope racing the car; highways roaring and his own voice, day after day, lecturing, mumbling, complaining. Behind him now, all of it. He hated the prospect of driving back to Kingston and the life, if one could call it that, of end-of-the-trail waiting. He made an effort. "Otis, I'm glad you're stepping out."

"It won't be a stroll in the park,"

"You'll be showing the flag, so to speak."

"Let's not get too dramatic."

"Why the hell not?"

Silence.

Otis said, "On second thought maybe dramatic is the way to go."

"Animals do it, running, soaring, growling, singing, showing off. We're animals too, we're species."

"Something's happened to you."

"Get on the road, old man. You'll find out."

The line hummed and Rufus smiled. He thought he knew what Otis would say next. But it was taking him a while. Come on, man.

"If you live long enough you get radical."

"Bingo."

"What?"

"Nothing. I was just agreeing with you."

"So, getting back to this geriatric bus."

"Give 'em hell, Otis. And you want this motel as a destination resort."

Otis chuckled. " Can you get that for us?"

"I think so. Here's what we've got here: ten or twelve units all in a row; wood construction, no plastic, no aluminum. Pines growing out back. It's called Quiet Pines."

"Good. Give me the phone number and could you rent about half the units for six months, with option to renew?"

"Okay. Give my regards to Maud and Sylvie and Babs and …"

"Herb."

"Yeah, Herb."

To: BREAKOUT@LISTSERV.SPEAKUP.ORG

From: mdel@yahoo.com

Re: Sharp-tail grouse

Met Rufus, heard about Breakout. Why couldn't he have told me Breakout has a listserv? I roved the internet, found you folks. Next day I had to take a plane to Omaha. (Family emergency, it turned out not too bad). Flying back, the plane passed fairly low over western Nebraska. It was early evening, the land full of gray and violet shadows, long humps and hollows and ridges, so mysterious and beautiful I fell in love with Nebraska all over again. Next free weekend I'll go looking for sharp-tailed grouse and other prairie inhabitants. I don't even know if sharp-tails are endangered. I grew up in the sand hills. I want to celebrate those birds, and the land.

Maureen

G rayling, Michigan.

Enid, having again re-scheduled her return flight to Wyoming, drove to New York's toll road and headed toward Grayling. Two days later, tired but happy, feeling she'd actually done some hands-on work for Breakout, she entered Grayling, examined buildings and yards, wanting everything to be just right. And there it was, Quiet Pines, its parking space bounded by small boulders and littered by fallen pine needles. Behind the motel grew tall pines, speckled and splotched by evening light. There was a strong woods turf scent that Enid caught as soon as she stepped out of the car.

She went into the office, tapped the little bell. A tall, stooped man entered, placed a pair of big hands flat on the counter and looked at Enid over the tops of glasses that were perched far down on his long beak. "You the lady Rufus is expecting?"

"Yes, how did you know?"

"Guessed. Not many customers these days. Rufus said you might be here about now. You want to go over the lease?"

I'm sure you and Rufus have that taken care of."

"It was a handshake deal," he said.

They studied each other. Enid said, "I'll endorse that," and held out her hand. His was thick-skinned and dry. She guessed he was a little younger than he looked. "Is Rufus here?"

"In Number Twelve, but I think he's out looking for those warblers." He reached to the key board, handed a key to her. It was attached to a substantial piece of pine.

"It's nice to have a real key," she said.

To: BREAKOUT@LISTSERV.SPEAKUP.ORG

From: fchavez@earthlink.com

Re: Butterfly

I work at Hal's Quick Stop, met a biker there, name of Wayne, told me about animals going extinct. Some right here in San Diego.

So, on our day off Dolores and I go to a place burned in last year's fires to look for tecate cypresses where Thorne's hairstreak butterflies live. We knew the fires might have burned up the last of them.

We met two other people. They were from the Center for Biodiversity and they were happy, they'd seen a few hairstreaks. They didn't want to show us where they were, but Dolores talked them into it. They showed us one butterfly and then we all went away from there. It was strange, seeing that insect, thinking only a few of them still alive, might go extinct any time, probably get hit by the next fire.

Cyber cafe, time running out. Here's Dolores.

That one butterfly we saw was beautiful. Wings of purple and white and orange. They need a new name. I'm glad we went there. Life is…oh, time's up.

D

Quiet Pines, Michigan.

Enid walked out bright and early,a little before sun-up, dressed in forest green cotton trousers and shirt to match and binoculars slung against her chest. A moment later the door of Number Twelve opened. Rufus, in loosely fitting bluejeans, yellow-and-green plaid shirt. And, of course, binoculars.

"Rufus?"

"Enid?"

They walked toward each other. Enid held out her arms. They hugged awkwardly, trying to keep binocs out of harm's way. Rufus said, "So, here we go again."

"Show me some birds."

They walked into the woods on a broad and winding path to a half-rotted plank bridge across a sluggish creek and alongside a small cattail marsh where rustling sounds stopped them.

Rufus said, "Wren."

The wren appeared, disappeared, appeared.

"Marsh wren," Enid said.

"Yup."

Suddenly the woods rang with the call of an ovenbird. They stood still and watched and found it, a feathered mite walking on a pine root, near enough to show the yellow-orange stripe on its crown.

They turned back toward the motel. Enid asked about Kirtland's warblers.

"I found some, I'll show you."

"Splendid. I suppose we ought to be talking business. There've been some developments."

"Coffee first. There's a place down the street."

They went to Rita's, took a table. Enid ordered toast and bacon, Rufus a short stack which he slathered with maple syrup and floated a square of butter on top. He sat back. "Grayling isn't too bad a place. I could spend my last days here." He chuckled. "Well, whoa there, I guess these *are* last days."

She let that pass. "Do you suppose it was a mistake to find a refuge so far north?"

"Cold winters."

"Yes."

"Oh I'd say that's the least of our worries." He dipped a spoon in his coffee, chased a bit of golden-brown foam and lifted it with exaggerated care. "Hah, gotcha. My gramma was good at this. Catch coffee foam, money's coming your way."

"We agreed to not worry about money," Enid said. "Remember?. Let me bring you up to date. What we started has gone off in different directions on its own, people talking to each other, some of them inventing actions. Like this amphibian network that started in Austin and now it's spread to Wyoming and Colorado and Wisconsin. And the Maple View people about to venture forth. That's scary, but I'm hopeful."

She held up a piece of toast, waggled it at him. "Grassroots democracy." She buttered the toast. "I also have some bad news. A few people posting on the Breakout list have been sending Jennifer and me backchannel stories abut being visited by federal security people, asking questions or handing out warnings."

"Looking for informers."

"Possibly."

"Cop types branded environmentalists as terrorists quite a while back, long before 9/11."

"And people believe it."

"Well, there are one or two enviro oufits that can be word-smithed just a bit, to fit the bill. Earth First! used to blockade roads, put their bodies on the line. I don't know what they're up to these days. And then there's the elves."

"Elves?"

"Earth Liberation Front. They're into infra-structure sabotage."

"I see. That gives the federals an edge."

"Sure, and there again, this is not new. The FeeBees and Red Squads, all those security types, they cast a wide net. It must be boring though, reading e-mails and documents, like in the big global monitor outfit in Virginia, or is it Maryland? I almost feel sorry for people in that kind of work. And then there's the ones who get to be outside knocking on doors, checking up on people, but where's the fun in it? Too easy to inject a little crystal of fear into a person, just by showing up and showing your ID. If that's all you can call your bundle of work for the day I should think you'd feel pretty dumb after a while. *Crystal of fear*. Otis thought that one up. Pretty good, eh?"

"Yes, it is. I did e-mail each person who has been visited, tried to reassure them, tried to be positive."

"Sure, that's all you can do."

"No, I don't think that's all we can do. I think we owe those people more than an e-mail or a phone call. I think we are obliged to be more personal and I'm not going to stand for our people going around scared. My big problem is that there's so much I don't know, about this nation of ours. about all of us. I feel sort of in the middle, Jennifer and Wayne on the younger side of me and you and Otis on the other."

"Otis and I are pretty damned old, Enid. I don't know if we can learn any new tricks."

"Old tricks, new tricks," she said, leaning toward him, "we have to use everything we can lay our hands on. And don't forget, young dogs have a lot to learn too."

"Try telling them that."

"Yes, well, let's return to a problem we might actually do something about."

"FeeBees and such."

"Yes." She cocked her head. "I know what you're thinking. You're thinking I take too much on myself."

"No, I'm thinking you can't stay away from a good fight."

"Really? Is it a good fight?"

He smiled. She wished he'd do that more often, it made him look mischievous. He said, "We'll find out."

"Could you travel for Breakout?"

"I guess you got me cornered. What kind of travel?"

"I have a list, six or seven names. I thought you might drop in on the three that happen to be in the eastern half of the country. Jennifer can talk Wayne into taking the others."

"FeeBee visitees?"

"Yes."

"Wayne'd be good at that. He ought to be paid too, top dollar, and expenses."

"Same goes for you. Equal work, equal pay. And Breakout will furnish you with a laptop."

"No, please, no laptop. I can fix a toaster, maybe a vacuum cleaner. Can't fix a damned computer."

"Are you serious? Everybody nowdays...oh all right, I won't argue. But we have to keep in touch, from now on. Do you have a cell phone?"

"No. Can't fix them either."

"I'll supply you with one. You have to accept it. Don't argue."

To: BREAKOUT@LISTSERV.SPEAKUP.ORG

From: lisaj@bayside.com

Re: Suisun Thistle

I too am concerned about the Suisun Thistle. Less than one acre in two locations constitutes its entire remaining habitat. It requires salty or brackish water, less human shifting of water levels and a firm halter on urban sprawl.

It's not a spectacular species; it doesn't lean to you to be petted. You can speak to it, but I doubt that it listens. It's just there. Gertrude Stein used to live here in the Bay Area. She said, "There's no there there." But there is.

Lisa

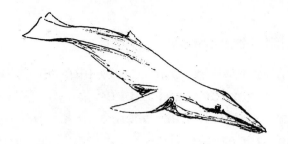

Sylvie sat up front, worn to a frazzle, but willing herself to stay awake, to watch land unroll as the bus ate the Interstate. Babs was asleep, across the aisle. So was Herb, three seats behind Babs. They looked like helpless rag dolls, mouths sagging, making little noises. From further back came low sounds of conversation, Otis and Maud. Sylvie wondered what those two found to talk about. Why were they talking at all instead of watching the outside, the away and away from Maple View?

Hardwood forest now, night closing in. Sylvie's thoughts turned to the sea, glamorous images of great seething waves and deep diving whales. She closed her eyes and the blue whale was there, steep slopes of its dark hide glistening wet. She felt a great truth, she and whales thousands of miles apart but sharing, negotiating moment by moment the world.

Time to wake Babs, time for her meds. When would Otis tell them where they were going?

Sybille canyon, Wyoming.

Jennifer walked out of the lab. She put both hands to her face and rubbed hard, then tossed her hair back. It had been an exhausting day, setting up a new batch of bacteria cultures, helping Steve and Lisa with routine chores, downloading recent research on rodent viral diseases. She watched shadows creep up the ridges, pushing light ahead of them. A motor roared on the highway, approaching from the south. Jennifer fantasized, forced the sound to be from Wayne's bike. A single headlight dipped around the bend. Jennifer tensed, the bike slowed, turned into the driveway and stopped and the rider lifted his helmet, his hair golden brown in the fading light. He propped the hog and took the parking area in long-legged strides.

"Wayne."

"Jennifer."

They collided. "Jenny," he whispered, but he broke their hard embrace, confused, worried.

"You never called me that," she said.

He looked down. "Lots of times, down in Arizona…California, Nevada, Utah…it's a big country."

They stood still, measuring each other. He said, "Hey, I been missing you."

"Let's walk."

"Sure. Been ridin' all day. Stiff as a board."

They jumped the creek, took the faint path that sometimes lost itself in creekside jungle. They slipped through to a little clearing that opened on a steep sagebrush slope. She turned and they reached for each other.

They couldn't pretend any longer.

To: BREAKOUT@LISTSERV.SPEAKUP.ORG

From: wiltol@erinet.com

Re: Greens

Almost everybody focuses on animals, forgetting the fundamental collusion between sun and plants. If there is anything sacred down here on this earth it is this green magic (red and blue too).

We can't save species, we can't save ourselves, without tender and loving and knowlegable care for the life giving source of all thundering herds on earth, and monster whales at sea.

You guys keep hammering on the need for habitats, for every species. That's essential, but habitats are not just any kind of extra space saved from the bulldozer. Habitats are where green stuff thrives in extraordinary, amazing, confusing diversity.

wt

The bus slowed, took an exit ramp, then an unpaved road, swaying and bumping, the headlights creating a tunnel through forest. Otis stood behind the driver, hanging onto the driver's seatback, bent forward, peering ahead. The driver murmured something. Otis nodded. The bus stopped and the headlights went out.

Otis said, "I think we've made our escape."

"I won't cheer just yet," Maud said

Otis said, "Let me introduce our driver, Leonard Aguillar."

The driver turned in his seat and faced them with a smile. "My job," he said, "is to get you to where you want to go. Where that is, I don't know."

"Otis knows," Herb said.

Otis glared at Herb and took a deep, slow breath. "Somebody had to make arrangements, Herb. We walked out of Maple View without giving notice, to put some distance between us and HMO lawyers. But we owe family members an explanation. That's for each one of us to take care of, first thing tomorrow. Make sure you contact somebody."

"I'm happy," Babs said.

Herb said, "And now, Otis, how about letting us in on where we're headed?"

"We have reservations, tomorrow night, High Tide Inn, Boothbay Harbor, Maine." He made his way to the back of the bus where, next to the john, a stash of blankets and pillows were heaped. "We're parked here to let the driver get some rest." Otis picked up a pillow and a pair of blankets and slumped into a rear seat. He adjusted it to full laid-back position and arranged his body for rest; for sleep, if the gods were kind.

Sylvie said, "Let's look for whales."

Maud groaned. "One thing at a time, Sylvie. Right now my job is getting this old body through this night."

To: eshaw@wyoming.com

From: jennf@ferrets.org

Re: FBI

Enid, When I was alone in Medicine Bow people there caught on quickly that I was a fugitive, and they tolerated me, even eventually came to a sort of passive support. But I couldn't confide in anyone there. Lonesome time. I'd known isolation before, especially in a pallid marriage, but that Medicine Bow winter was a long tough haul.

You know, Enid, there are times when I look at those ferrets and wonder why we bother. Born in captivity, they have to be trained, to kill. We teach them to be suspicious. Oh they move beautifully, but what are they thinking about? The scientist in me says, be patient, don't go off into wild speculation. But I can't resist wild speculation. My inner self-centered me asks what I think I'm doing up here in this canyon caring for these beady-eyed beasts? The Breakout in me says, Hey, our species is on the move. In that moving is where I feel most at home.

FBI? They're pretty low on my worry list.

Thanks for listening.   Jenny

Leonard hung back, took an interest in a scale model of a three-masted ship, or schooner, whatever. His passengers were moving slowly along High Tide Inn's breakfast buffet. "What a bunch of old crows I got landed with," Leonard was thinking. But they were interesting. There would be trouble, of course. He'd known that when he'd grabbed the chance for a change in the usual routine of driving a tour bus crammed with tourists bound and determined to have the time of their life, the whole gaggle headed by a leader of the domineering type, male or female. Necessary talent, Leonard admitted. You couldn't move a bunch of strangers into and out of places and come back with full count, if you didn't have Alpha wolf mentality. Otis, old man, no alpha wolf, but he was trying hard. Leonard bent closer to the deck of the model, admired the anchor chain made of fine wire. Making that chain must have used up an evening or two.

Maud called to him, insisting he join them. Nice of her. He went to the buffet. Boiled eggs, muffins, toast, butter, jelly, cold cereal, milk, hot cakes, syrup, sprigs of parsley, coffee, real cream. Not bad, this job, not bad at all, so far.

The tide was out. Otis stepped with care down the ramp to the floating docks where big private boats were tethered. The docks moved, ever so slightly. Stay alert, new territory here, this isn't a Maple View hallway. One of the boats was named Jenny II. Well, what do you know? Favorable omen from Sybille canyon? It pleased him to think so.

He put a hand against the hull, but the boat was making little lifting motions not quite in sync with the dock beneath his feet. He felt queasy. He walked on. A sleek boat was heading seaward from the far side of the harbor. There were people on board behind glass windows, doing nothing. Whale watchers? He raised his binoculars. The bow of the boat had a small bone in its teeth and the name was *Harbor Princess*. Would it be all right to put Sylvie on board such a boat and bill Breakout? Who ought to decide such a question? Should every little item be subject to discussion? Where draw the line? Otis. for god sake, quit thinking.

He heard shouting. At the top of the ramp, Herb and the driver, Herb doing the shouting.

Otis cupped his good ear, caught a few words. "Whale...dead whale..."

Leonard drove the bus on a narrow highway that wound past modest and not so modest seaside homes backed by forest. Gradually the houses became scarcer. The car ahead dipped out of sight. Leonard braked, unwilling to commit. A van had been tail-gating the bus; it gave a long bleat, but Leonard put on his blinkers and slowed to a stop. Another long complaint from the van. Leonard ignored it as he surveyed the dirt turn-off into a sandy cove flooded with sunlight and bounded by low rock ledges still wet from the night's high tide. On the beach a crowd of people. The cove was jammed with parked vehicles. Leonard didn't want to put the bus down there. Too much sand, not enough turning space. The sea was calm and glittering.

Babs shrieked. "There it is, oh my god."

"This is as far as we go," Leonard said, as he moved the bus to the shoulder. That was sandy too. Leonard kept the lefthand tires on the black-top. The van bleated its displeasure.

Sylvie had already taken position at the bus entrance, hanging onto the steel pole with both hands. She started down the steps. Leonard opened the door and the full force of the stench of rotting flesh rolled into the bus. The tail-gater van tried to edge around the bus, but its driver suddenly turned cautious, braked, reversed, parked behind the bus.

Leonard opened the door. Babs and Sylvie exited, started down the sandy slope, supporting each other. Maud followed, then Otis and Herb. Otis noticed a black and red logo on the side of the van. DOWNEAST TV. He remarked to Herb, "This is not good."

"I have to agree," Herb said.

Two men sidled past them, lugging TV gear. Herb stopped, positioned his cane, took a backword glance. He nudged Otis. "Don't look now, a pair of cops talking to Leonard."

Otis looked. "State troopers. Now we're boxed in, rats in a trap. Shouldn't have let Sylvie talk us into this."

"Speaking of whom," Herb replied, "there she is, out in the wet sand, right up there with those two guys doing something with the whale."

"My guess is they're some kind of biologists, doing some kind of autopsy."

"Could be."

"What about those cops?"

"Don't ask me. I'm no longer taking the lead, Herb."

"Democracy now?"

"You got it."

The men at the whale were biologists, as Otis had surmised. They motioned to Sylvie to stand back. One of them said, "We're trying to determine cause of death."

Sylvie wasn't listening. She was trying to look the whale in the eye, an eye gritty with sand, half shut, dead. A large whale, Sylvie didn't know its species name; names didn't matter, not now in these few moments alone with sea and whale. The autopsy men, and Bab's begging her to get back from that stinking dead thing, came to her as distant disturbances in the slow sluicing of ocean water on rock and sand.

A few people, muttering about not being able to breathe the sickening stink any longer, began to leave, but they stopped to watch the state cops advance down the slope in a half trot.

Sylvie rejoined Babs and Maud. The TV guys, looking for local color, chose the three stubborn old women who stood at the very front of the crowd, on the line between dry and wet, and now the troopers entered the frame, going immediately to those three old women, and now a pair of geezers joined the women and a trooper was addressing one of the geezers.

"Sir, your name please."

"Otis Rameau."

"And you reside at Maple View Care Center."

"How do you know that?"

"A Kingston, New York request. We ran the plates on your bus, made inquiries, spoke to your driver."

The other cop began to question Babs. She shouted in his face, furious and afraid. "No, I'm not going back, no way, go away."

"Ma'am, if you will come with us to the station, we'll get this whole matter straightened out."

Maud said, "We escaped, we walked out of Maple View perfectly peacefully and within our rights and we had help from Breakout for which I for one am eternally grateful."

"Breakout?" The trooper was smiling, but no one was leaving.

"Ma'am, we will have to ask you a few questions. Let's do it privately. All right?"

"I don't choose private," Maud shouted. "Breakout is about life on this earth, life for whales and...butterflies, and people too."

She stopped to draw breath. Babs took over. "We left Maple View because we thought it would be better for us to go out to help. It wasn't only personal reasons."

The TV camera was taking it all in, its two handlers beaming, happy as clams.

The crowd buzzed. Someone shouted, "Where did you escape from?" Maud laughed. She had recovered, ready for battle. "Nursing Home," she shouted back.

More camera work as Otis proclaimed that Breakout was about living with life's diversity instead of ripping it off. "We're travelers, looking for ways to help in that...struggle."

Herb, tumbling to the fact that he and his fellow travellers were news in the making, grinned happily and put a hand on Otis's shoulder and the other on Maud's. The two troopers looked at each other, the TV camera rolled on, the biologists stopped work, the crowd closed in and a man in a tee shirt and black denim pants and navy blue cap shouldered his way forward. "We'll take you on, Breakout. We can use any help you have on offer. I am George Kelly. I represent *Maine Sea Turtle Watch*."

Otis reached past a woman who held a camera equipped with a huge telephoto lens. He grasped the sea turtle man's hand. "We can talk about that. Let me introduce our little group here."

One of the troopers leaned closer to Otis. "Hold on, sir, not so fast. Let's everybody calm down."

His partner repeated that all could be satisfactorily settled back at the station, but the sea turtle man said, "I think we'd all like to know what these people are charged with."

The trooper quelled his anger, with difficulty. "Routine inquiry, no charge, as yet."

The woman with the telephoto said, "You have to give these people a reason, don't you? Or is this some kind of Patriot Act move you're trying to ram through here?"

Murmurs in the crowd. Someone yelled, "You're in Maine, a free state."

The TV camera was still alive, it's eye relentlessly roving from speaking face to speaking face. The two troopers looked at each other, eyebrows questioning.

Sylvie said, "Look at the whale," Her voice, though low and plaintive, carried well, and most of the people did shift their gaze to the huge body. The camera, after a slight hesitation, turned seaward and for a fleeting few moments the only sounds came from restless sea and a few gulls soaring low, waiting their turn.

A voice from the crowd. " Let's have some law and order here and I don't mind saying I support the Patriot Act."

Another voice. "I say let these people go."

George Kelly raised his right hand high and turned his body as he spoke. "In Maine we've been getting on just fine with common sense for a couple centuries. Common sense, it's a heritage."

The woman with the telephoto locked arms with Maud who, startled for a moment, took Sylvie's arm in hers. Indecisiveness ruled the crowd and for a few blinks took hold of the troopers too. One of the TV reporters, backstepping toward the whale, addressed the troopers. "Officers, it's in the can ready for six o'clock news. I'm pretty sure the station can supply you with a complete copy." His tone changed as he posed hmself to speak directly into the TV lens. "I'm on a beach a few miles north of Boothbay Harbor where the mystery of a whale's death is under investigation. We'll report further developments as they occur."

The troopers consulted each other, then one of them spoke to Otis, asking for his address.

"Maple View Care Center."

"Yes, we have that. And what is the street and zip?"

Otis stared into the trooper's youngish brown eyes, trying to remember Maple Field's zip.

Maud came up with it.

"Right, thank you Ma'am. Let's step aside for a few minutes."

Maud hesitated, looked at Otis, then Herb. She turned back to the trooper. "We're not going to the station."

"I believe that's what we're agreeing to here," the trooper said, with a quick look at his partner, who gave back a hairbreadth shrug.

Maud led to a lone pine just above high tide line. Her comrades followed. The crowd began to break up, not before snapping photos of the Breakout Five, the TV men, the cops. The woman with the telephoto switched lenses adjusted speed and apperture, handed the camera to George Kelly. She stood against sea and whale, arms crossed, looking severe. George aimed and fired.

A big man in heavy wool sweater, whipcord pants and rubber boots came from the jam of vehicles at a slow jog. "George," he said, "what did I miss out on?"

"Didn't you get my message?"

"I did, but I was at the hardware, customers stacked up three deep. George, you have to get over this mumbling on the phone. I thought you had a stranded turtle."

"No, just a whale.

"I see the TV is here."

"Sure is, getting a nice little story. See those folks over there? They're from an outfit called *Breakout*. We can talk with them, about help, maybe about money."

Dennis's weather-cracked mouth widened, showing a beautiful set of teeth. "The Lord moves in mysterious ways, His marvels to perform."

To: BREAKOUT@LISTSERV.SPEAKUP.ORG

From: bconner@earthlink.com

Re: amphibians

Cerise, Brian, Jason and all:

Frogs, and ampibians in general, are exposed to just about everything out there.

Take leopard frogs, /Rana pipiens/. Recent experiments show at least two known causes for limb abnormalities. One is infection by a parasite, the other is the weedkiller component, Atrazine When both parasites and Atrazine are present in water where tadpoles are growing, the number of abnormalities increases. Furthermore, Atrazine in very, very small doses (as low as 0.2 parts per billion), can cause male frog gonads to become hermaphroditic, producing eggs as well as sperm.

(Does this have anything to do with low sperm counts in human males?). I got all this data from Rachel Carson Council. Bert

Jonesport, Maine.

A cool wind from the surfaces of a calm harbor brought powerful odors of tidal zone to the lobby of the Four Seasons Motel. Leonard, happy to have been invited to the confab, tipped his chair against the wall and let his eyelids droop . The conversation soothed him into a doze.Talk of sea turtles and fishes, plankton and whales, ocean currents, global warming, depressed towns, wimpy politicians, all blended into a music of ebb and flow, until Otis's voice rose into a shout. Leonard jerked, opened his eyes.

Otis was on his feet, precariously, one hand clumsily grabbing at the soft, fake leather arm of one of the Motel's old sofas. "No, no and no. Breakout is not about prefabricated letters to congress persons."

"Well then, what *is it about*," George asked.

"It's a work in progress." Otis let himself fall back into the squish of the sofa. "Oh hell, I'm sorry, George, I'm dead tired, we all are, didn't mean to get aggressive."

Dennis said, "George, we'd best get on home. Gig tomorrow."

"Not till we talk about money."

"We're frazzled old rag dolls," Babs said. "Can't we talk tomorrow? What's your gig?"

"Contra dance, without the piano. He quit."

George balked at the word *quit*. "Arthritis got too bad, not his fault, he and wife went to Arizona."

Dennis said, "We had us a vocalist once."

"I was a vocalist, once," Maud said, "couple of centuries ago. Garage band, bunch of high school kids, I sang my heart out."

They all turned to her, surprised. She laughed softly, having caught them trying to travel the back trail that would replace her smooth helmet of pure gray, delicate dewlaps, pouched cheek flesh. They failed, of course. But her voice, deep, hardly a quaver, gave everyone pause.

"Hey, don't get worried, guys. I'm not looking for an audition."

But George couldn't help being interested. "You know that song Willie Nelson sang at the closing of the winter Olympics?"

She said, "I love that song."

Rufus sat on a fairly comfortable chair just inside the open doorway of his unit at Quiet Pines, inhaling the piney scent, savoring the warmth and the light. A squirrel was chattering. The phone rang. Rufus groaned, levered himself out of the chair, picked up.

Otis. "Did you see us on TV?"

"I did, just by chance. My landlord did too. Now he wants to know everything about Breakout Travelers."

"Did you rent those units?"

"Yes, all settled. Back to the whale scene, it was great, put you on the map."

"Put Breakout out there, yes, and that's what we want. Thanks for getting us a headquarters. Right now we're based at a motel in Jonesport. That's in Maine. Seems we've signed up in the entertainment business, traveling, putting on dances. Remember those sea turtle guys? One of them was on the TV. Dennis plays guitar, George on fiddle. They pick up local talent wherever they can. Enid sent some Breakout money. We're doing little jobs, helping one way or another. Babs came up with this idea of copying that Houston toad single sheet idea. So, we printed up a big pack of Sea Turtle sheets, hand them out at dances and other places."

"These turtle guys, are they okay to work with?"

"Yeah, we get along pretty good. They're recently retired, live at poverty level, have families here in Jonesport."

"When do you show up in Grayling?"

"Don't know, I'll keep in touch."

"I might not be here. Enid gave me an assignment."

"Do I get to hear about it?"

"Sure. I'll be dropping in on a few Breakout people who've been visited by Homeland Security types."

"Ah yes, FeeBees, back to their old routines."

To: eshaw@wyoming.com

From: pgall@jerseycom.com

Re: Help

Dear Enid Shaw, When I saw the TV spot about Otis and the others at that dead whale I couldn't help being envious. That's where I and Helen and Sam ought to be: free, out there doing things. We're not quite dead yet and man, I'm telling you, we have oceans of time that could be put to good use.

This is hard for me to do, to beg, but I'm going to do it. Could Breakout get us three out of Harbor View? In return we would do whatever needs doing that's within our power. Just ask, we would try. All we need is a vehicle and a very small bit of cash. There, I've said it. You'll turn us down, probably. That's okay, we understand, but I just had to try.

Sincerely yours, Paul Gallegos 028-774-2178

Jonesport, Maine.

The Breakout bus returned from a Friday dance at the student union in Orono and a Saturday night dance in Houlton. Attendance had been good, and many sea turtle singles had been distributed. When the bus parked at Four Seasons Motel, George and Dennis went home to their families and the others retired to their rooms, exhausted. Except Leonard, who strolled along the wharves, talking with fishermen, showing curiosity, inviting comments on sea life, lobster traps, boats and gear. He breathed deeply of seaweed odors, glad to be on his own for a while.

Otis snoozed until evening, then went looking for Herb. found him on a bench overlooking the harbor. "Not too bad a day."

"Yeah. Those gulls sure make a racket."

"I'm thinking it's time we get on up to Michigan. What do you think?"

Herb shrugged, looked sour, but the antagonism between him and Otis had undergone a sea change since they had weathered the beached whale crisis and ventured on with George and Dennis in the forests and on the coastlines of Maine, listening to tall tales from the two stalwart defenders of sea-going turtles. The stories were somewhat overdrawn accounts of real adventures, nearly always something strange or hilarious became the pole around which narratives unwound. Many a mile of Maine highways had passed like that, sometimes both Herb and Otis laughing at the same turn of phrase or hard-to-believe occurance.

Otis said, "I'm thinking maybe we could talk Dennis and George into going with us."

"Grayling is a long way from tidewater."

"I know that, but why not bring ocean news inland? Still a bunch of sea turtle singles to get rid of. You want to go talk to them?"

"Why me?"

"Grassroots Democracy, Herb. Tasks get spread around."

To: BREAKOUT@LISTSERV.SPEAKUP.ORG
From: lgarcia@yahoo.com

Re: Endangered Species Act

What counts is how the ESA is activated. What happened in San Diego can serve as a lesson. I'll report on only one piece of the mish-mash of city, county, federal, environmental and business people's creation, a Habitat Conservation Plan.

Fairy shrimp, tadpole shrimp, mesa mint and other at-risk plants and animals live in depressions that spring rains fill with water: "vernal pools." Dozens of these pools were located and studied by biologists, on the site of the proposed Mira Mesa Market center. The Habitat Conservation plan envisioned a trade-off between profit needs of developers and life sustaining needs of species. Some of the vernal pools were to be saved as functioning biological components of the market center.

However, vision has to be backed by hard language and that's where the consensus agreement failed. Its wording was fuzzy. Key provisionss were undercut by phrases such as "avoid to the maximum extent practicable." The result, at Mira Mesa? All but one pool was bulldozed and that one is now surrounded by the shopping center and apartment complex.. During most of the year the pool looks like a bit of waste land left over from construction. Some of the people living there don't even know there is life there.

This is only part of what went on in the San Diego area. The story can stand as a symbol of our society cowtowing to market forces. What are market forces? Dare we look them in the face?

This pool scene at Mira Mesa is kinda like a zoo, no connectivity with natural habitats. Part of its circumference is an iron fence. I'm not kidding. Go there, see for yourself. Worse than a zoo, there is no keeper. Not even a sign to tell people the story.

Lorie

Herb reported to Otis. "They're rarin' to go. Chance to see some country, chance to take sea turtle news inland, chance to get away from home a while. In order of priority."

Otis smiled. "George and Dennis, they are something else. When do we hoist sail for Grayling?"

"Tomorrow okay?"

"Have to have a meeting, get everybody's agreement."

"Oh yeah, democracy, I almost forgot."

Grayling, Michigan.

Albert Ferguson, realtor, parked his Honda at Quiet Pines, next to the Breakout bus and went into the office. He tapped the bell, waited impatiently. "Harvey, you home?" He smelled pancakes and honey.

Harvey Boshardt shuffled through the inner doorway.

"Ferguson said. "I need to talk to you."

"Go ahead."

"I can come back later if you're having breakfast."

"No, just washing dishes." He gave Ferguson a steady stare. He knew the man, but realtors were not his favorite kind of person.

Ferguson leaned on the counter and spoke in a low voice. "This Breakout bunch you're putting up here. Know much about them?"

"Don't need to know."

Ferguson chuckled, his jowels jiggling. "You like the color of their money."

Harvey shrugged, held the stare.

"Breakout is very likely a front."

"Sure, it's a front for endangered species. Rufus told me the whole story, and it's on their website."

"Yes, yes, I know, that's their side of it. The other side is a bit darker."

"Darker." Harvey nearly smiled. "You mean the terrist thing."

"Precisely. Now, I'm here on behalf of Homeland Partnerships? Homeland security and private businesses and individuals getting together for the good of the country."

"Oh, I see. Socialism."

Ferguson reared back. "What? Oh, joke. Well, well, Harvey, that's a new side of you. Seriously, I'm involved. Enough said."

"What do you want, Al?"

"Could you get me in with these Breakout people?"

"Al, for god sake, all you have to do is walk up to them. They're a bunch of old geezers and gals and they like to talk. You don't need an intro from me. If you do get in you'd have to go knocking on doors, hand out these things." He reached into the shelf under the counter, came up chuckling, handed Ferguson a stiff paper, a handout about sea turtles, written by Dennis and George of Maine Sea Turtle Watch, decorated in two colors by Eleanor, George's wife.

Ferguson studied it, shaking his head slowly. "I can do that, if I have to. Now, to get to the point, I hear that your people here are about to travel. I want to go along."

"Al, look, they're not *my people*. They're guests."

"Right, of course. Who's in charge of these guests?"

"Al, that's enough. I'm not opening up my books to you. If you want to pick a bird or turtle or butterfly you're interested in, I can let them know. Like, you explore swamps looking for water snakes."

Ferguson said. "Thanks, Al. I owe you one."

"Uh huh. Well then, what's your animal?"

"My animal? Like a password?"

"I don't know, but I think they all have favorites. The little woman with the sharp nose, sharp eyes, she's into whales."

Ferguson said, "Help me out."

"You fish don't you? Fish are animals."

"Why yes, of course."

"Pick an endangered one."

"Oh, right. Sturgeon."

To: BREAKOUT@LISTSERV.SPEAKUP.ORG

From: ghart@earthlink.com

Re: Hogs and Chickens

Dear thoughtful friends, I want to ask why we can't get a little upset about hogs kept in cages measuring 2 feet by 3 feet by 7 feet, until they are knocked on the head and shipped to slaughter. And laying hens in cages so small they often walk on each other. No dust to bathe in. I'm not saying animals have rights or do not have rights. As a longtime subscriber to /Environmental Ethics/ I'm acquainted with "rights" talk and have decided that rights talk doesn't apply very well at all to our relations with nature. Nature's too complicated.

However, I'm here to say I feel bad about factory farming. Somehow I don't feel right about it.

Gary :(

Al Ferguson rang the bell, stood back one step and looked across the street, saw that Babs and Sylvie were engaged in what looked like an earnest conversation with a woman in a hair net. She, arms akimbo, leaned against the doorjamb as though she had time to spare. Babs was laughing.

"She busts out every ten minutes," Ferguson thought, but he had to admit she was no clothhead. On the bus ride into this Grayling suburb, where Ferguson hoped nobody would recognize him, he had seated himself up front, behind the driver, wanting a quick jump start in his mission, knowing that the driver had been with this Breakout crew for a while: prime source of information.

But Babs, across the aisle, had started grilling him, putting him through a gauntlet of personal questions. Are you married? What does your wife do? Where's she from? Are you happy with your work? That one, about happiness, backed by a half smile on Babs' face, had riled Ferguson and he'd come close to getting up and telling her to mind her own business, but his mind had stalled on *happiness*, telling hm he was sick and tired of pretending to be a jolly, middle-aged American forging ahead, taking obstacles in stride, bouncing back. Only last night he and Marie had gone through pending real estate prospects and Ferguson had noticed how pleased Marie was, looking forward to being in full charge of the business. He knew she'd do well at it; she was a natural, would probably end July with the business high up in the black, might even get the dinosaur off their hands, that fallen down lakeside cottage with rotting wharf and no indoor plumbing.

But Al had handled Babs with hearty guffaws, hard slap on his thigh, topping it off with a wink and, "You really want to know?"

The door opened, a weary old man in a bathrobe stood blinking in the light.

Ferguson opened with, "Hello, only a moment of your time, I have something for you."

"I'm not buying."

Ferguson stood there tongue-tied. He couldn't believe it; he knew every trick of his trade, even those that some of his colleagues thought were sure grabbers and that Ferguson had tried and found wanting; he knew opening phrases and closing phrases and everything in between. People management, that was his life. But now he stood facing the mild stare of a stranger and holding a bundle of Sea Turtle paper in his hands, speechless. He held out a single sheet. It was accepted. "Sea turtles? What's that got to do with Michigan?"

Ferguson heard himself say that marine life was an important issue. "What you have there is a small handful of vital information about sea turtles. And I thank you for your time." He stepped back, expecting the door to close, and knowing he was disregarding Otis's earnest advice: "Don't just hand them out. These are not throwaways. Engage in conversation."

The old man's glasses glinted as he held the turtle sheet to catch the light. "That's pretty good work. Who did it?"

"Breakout," Ferguson replied, as his peripheral vision caught Sylvie and Babs on the sidewalk on their way to the next house. Ahead of him.

"No, I don't mean some damn organization. What person did this? You?"

"No, not me. Some folks back in Maine. They're very concerned there, about sea turtles" Ferguson was getting it all wrong and knew it.

"I see the drawing is signed," the man said, holding the sheet close, studying Eleanor's tiny signature. "A woman's name, looks like. You'd never guess I used to draw, all the time, all kinds of things. I was good at it."

"I'm sure you were."

"Sold some." he shook his head. "Clip art, a sideline of course. Worked at River Rouge back then." He sighed. "Time marches on. I'll read this, later. Have a good day." The door closed.

Ferguson hustled to the next house. The door was open, the room empty. Hard rock hammered, muffled by walls. Ferguson pounded on the door jamb. A young man appeared. Baggy jacket, ultra-baggy pants, sulky face. Early teens. He said, "Nobody's home."

"But you are, my man," said Ferguson, grinning, He offered a turtle sheet. The kid took it, dropped it casually. It fluttered to the carpet.

"All right Buster," Ferguson said, "if that's your attitude." He stooped, grabbed the sheet and turned away with a parting shot. "Time to grow up, fella."

The kid's slamming of the door was punctuated by a scream from across the street, and Sylvie's high pitched voice calling for help. Ferguson ran to where Sylvie was kneeling on a lawn next to Babs who lay stretched full length, not moving. A man in shirtsleeves leaned over them, his voice loud in the quiet street. "You all right, you all right?"

Sylvie snarled at him. "No, she's not all right you goddamn beast."

Babs struggled to a sitting position. She looked alarmingly blank, but her fingers were busy, searching her scalp. She found the hurt place, pressed it and fell back in pain.

Sylvie said, "Don't move, lie still, everything's going to be all right."

Ferguson arrived, breathing hard. He took off his lightweight summer jacket and folded it into a pillow. Sylvie held Babs' head while Ferguson placed the jacket. He became aware of someone at his left shoulder, the sulky kid.

"She might be concussed," Sylvie said. "She's got to get to a doctor."

Ferguson punched the kid on the arm. "Go, call 911."

The kid shouldered past the hovering man, up the steps and into the house. The hovering man said, "I didn't do a thing, not one godamn thing. She fell, that's all."

"Yes, she fell," hissed Sylvie, "and you were saying bad things at us, poking your finger in our face and Babs stepped back and fell off your goddamn porch. You call that nothing?"

The man reared to his full height, his finger stabbed again. "I was talking to you two women, that's all, telling you where to get off. You couldn't take it could you? Couldn't take a little wake-up call. My son's in the military, ready to defend our country and people like you go creeping around undermining everything this country stands for."

"I can understand that," Ferguson said, "but right now we've got to make sure this lady here gets medical attention."

The kid bounced down the steps. "They're on their way."

"Thanks," Ferguson said.

They waited for the medics, the householder on the steps, head in his hands, talking, low-voiced now, about his infantry son; Ferguson next to him, listening; Babs on the ground still as a mouse, but breathing regularly; Sylvie on her knees next to Babs; the kid standing hipshot, reading about sea turtles.

To: BREAKOUT@LISTSERV.SPEAKUP.ORG

From: dhoffer@yahoo.com

Re: Barn door skate

They undulate along sea floors in the Gulf of Maine and further south off New England coast. They can grow to more than four feet long. Related to sharks.

Their numbers have declined. One theory holds that they are on the brink of extinction. But other studies claim that, though in low numbers, the population is stable. Another view is that our methods of sampling the skates are crude; we don't really know the true size of the population. A fourth theory tries to look at the entire offshore ecosystem, noticing that overfishing of cod and haddock and other large fish sent repercussions vibrating all up and down the food chain, favoring some smaller fish that formerly served as food for the bigger species. Smaller fish, either of the same species or of differing species have an advantage here: they can feed on small animals, such as various worms and crustaceans. Bigger individuals need larger prey and so, for them, starvation. The barn door skate, largest of the six or seven species of Atlantic coast skates, might be seriously short of food.

I like number four, because it tries to look at the whole system, but admit that it needs more material evidence to become full fledged.

There's a lesson here: lack of knowledge. On the other hand, we can't blindly ignore what we do know with reasonable certainty. We do know that oceans are in deep trouble: rising sea levels, shifts in currents, temperature changes, overfishing, etc.   In a halfway rational society this knowledge would be taken seriously, while at the same time admitting we don't know enough to manage the world. As a sensible species, we would give ourselves lots of slack by being cautious. We might tear down mistakes, such as mega dams and stream straightenings, give life back to the salmon others, the eel others, the life in oceans and fresh waters about which we know not nearly enough.

Sorry to run on so long, but the knowlege situation is one terrific and terrifying message we can deliver to the national debate.

Doris

They met in the bus, Otis facing them from the front, standing on the next to last entrance step; Leonard, in the driver's seat, skewed around to face Otis; Sylvie and Babs in the front seats; Maud behind them, by herself, and Herb, across the aisle from Maud; George and Dennis and Ferguson further back.

Otis opened the meeting. "We have an invitation from a Maureen Delacorte in Chadron,

Nebraska. She's organizer for something called Sharp-tail Grouse Festival. She wants us to put on a dance. The date is Saturday, August 6. What's our pleasure?"

Sylvie said, "Babs needs more rest. It's only two days since her fall."

Babs reared up in a rare objection to mothering. "I'm okay."

"You might be concussed."

"I'm not concussed, doctor told me so."

"You need rest."

"Sylvie, for god sake, lay off will you?"

Sylvie obeyed.

Silence, Otis waiting.

George and Dennis looked at each other. George said, "There's a little problem. For a dance you need music. A fiddle and a guitar do not a terrific dance band make."

"Why can't you find local talent," Maud asked, "like you were always doing in Maine?"

Neither George nor Dennis wanted to chance it. "We know Maine," Dennis said. "We don't know Nebraska."

Otis said, "Okay, I'll call this Maureen person, tell her we can't oblige."

"Wait," Sylvie said. "We could put an ad on the Breakout list."

"We'd want somebody who can pitch right in," George said, "somebody experienced."

"But not some concert perfectionist," Dennis added.

To: BREAKOUT@LISTSERV.SPEAKUP.ORG.

From: vlentz@fastnet.com

Re: War

You enviro people have your heads in the sand. People are dying for no good reason, all over the world. I'm a hunter and I kill for my family and I was in Vietnam, plenty old enough now to look back on useless killing and it's still going on. Stupid. Heartless.

We all die. But dying while carrying out wrong orders from wrong-headed members of our sad species is no way to go. Young people, ours and the others, limbless. What do you say to them? I'm asking you: WHAT DO YOU SAY TO THEM?

This list is supposed to be about endangered species. Well, who's more endangered than people? There's only one way out, we have to quit war, cold turkey. Just DO IT. I'm so mad I could chew natils.   Volmar

Quiet Pines. Fireflies sparked the darkness. Babs, Maud, Sylvie, Leonard and Herb sat around a small table in Babs' room playing five card draw. In Otis's unit, George, Dennis and Otis had turned on the new laptop that had arrived that morning, shipped Fed-Ex by Breakout.

The laptop's server was refusing to respond. Otis, desperately sleepy and disgusted, sat back, drowsily listened to George and Dennis trying this and then that. Otis growled, "Get Sylvie." For a few moments a stab of nostalgia struck Otis as he recalled the balky old Mac dinosaur and Sylvie's way with it, and the very feel of Maple View. Long time ago.

George went away, returned with Sylvie. When she saw the computer she said, "Oh, lovely," and sat down and put her hands on the keyboard. She studied the screen. The three men formed a hovering cluster around her and waited. She re-started, removed the disk, held it to the lamp light. She reinserted it and began to work the keys. Windows came and went.

"Password," she said.

"Uh, we already put that in," Dennis said.

"Give it to me again."

He spelled it: GRAYL.

She smiled. "Easy to remember." Her fingers flashed and there it was: confirmation. She called for mail. One message.

To: BREAKOUT@LISTSERV.SPEAKUP.ORG

From: howie@midwest.com

Re: Music.

Saw your request on Breakout list. Have piano, will travel.

Howie

"That settles it," George said. "We go to Nebraska."

"That we do," Dennis said, "and with turtle singles."

Sylvie sat back, tired and bright-eyed. "Let's talk Maud into singing."

The others looked doubtful. Sylvie insisted. "She's good. I've heard her humming tunes. Sometimes she breaks out...I'm telling you, she has a voice."

The doubt lingered, Sylvie felt it, a mist, a miasma that clung. She leaned forward, put a white fist on the table. Her face had turned hard, her fist trembled, she looked at each of the men in turn, demanding attention. She said, "Otis, you're always talking about breaking new ground."

"Yes," he admitted.

"Well?"

George and Dennis looked at each other. "Dare to live," Dennis said.

Burlington, Vermont.

Sunset blazed behind the distant city center and there was a sheen of color across a sizeable lawn that flanked both sides of the house and rolled on to finally end at a beech/maple woodlot.

Rufus pressed the doorbell button. A catbird meowed, he looked for it, the door opened. The woman looked harried. "Yes?"

"I'm Rufus Knutson, from Breakout."

"Never heard of it, and I'm busy."

"I was just wondering if I might speak to Charlie. This is the Anderson residence, isn't it?"

"What is it you want?"

"A computer matter, nothing alarming."

She stood aside. "He's in the basement, practically lives down there." She opened a door and called out. "Charlie? A gentleman to see you, some computer business."

A muffled and laconic voice drifted up the stairs. "Send him down."

"I don't see why you can't get away long enough to come up and speak to the man."

"I'm in the middle of something."

The woman shook her head, sighed, turned to Rufus. "Would you mind?"

Rufus thanked her and went down basement steps that were covered in green industrial carpeting. The concrete floor was covered with the same stuff. In a far corner a young man sat under a bullet lamp, a book on his lap.

Rufus said, "Charlie? I'm Rufus Knutson, from Breakout. Maybe this isn't a good time?"

Charlie held up the book. "*Story of Pi.* I've got another forty-five pages to go."

"Good reading?"

"Yeah, it's interesting. A full-grown Bengal tiger on a raft in the ocean with this guy named Pi."

"And you have an assignment."

"Right, how'd you know?"

"Just guessing. You counted pages."

Charlie put the book aside. "The paper's due tomorrow. So, what's your problem?"

"If *you* don't have a problem, there is no problem. I'm here to talk, that's all, listen to whatever you might want to say, about that visit from federal security."

After only a few moments of hesitation Charlie got up and went to his computer. "I'll show you my e-mail to Breakout." He sat and poked the machine and it woke up. "It's what came into my mind just then; that's the way I write. When you write in cyberspace you don't have to make a big deal out of it. There it is." He got up and motioned to the empty chair. Rufus sat and read.

To: BREAKOUT@LISTSERV.SPEAKUP.ORG

From: cander@yahoo.com

Re: Amphibians

Some species will die out, it's inevitable. Others will be taken care of after the revolution.

     C.A.

Rufus said, "This means you have no serious commitment to endangered species."

Charlie was back in his armchair. "I'm a surfer, mainly. There's so much bullshit out there, you know. I'm into music and movies; I collect CDs, download stuff. I tried chatting for a while, wasn't my thing. I play video games. Serious commitment, well that has to do with the high school work. Awesome, the stuff they expect you to do."

"That word *revolution*. Just popped into your mind and you put it down, didn't think too much about it."

"Yeah, I know, that's what brought the feds to my door, that's what you're saying."

"You don't need me to tell you that."

"True."

Rufus decided there wasn't much more to do here; this kid didn't seem to be in much trouble. If he was, it certainly didn't show.

Charlie said, "People don't really understand the internet; it's a place where you bump into people and then move on; you might meet something interesting, or a person who's interesting and you keep in touch, but you stay on the move. That's the point of it; nobody's hanging over you. I'm not a joiner. I posted that e-mail to Breakout and moved on." He was looking at Rufus now, full in the face, being serious.

"I see," Rufus said. He groped for something more. "I'm an old fart, the internet is terra incognito to me; you're an explorer, way out there. But thanks for the intro. Maybe I'll try it myself before cashing in my chips, but this past year I've been having a strong yen to get down to Costa Rica."

"Costa Rica?"

"To see birds, that's *my* serious thing."

Charlie was relaxing now. "Hey, don't you know you could call up Costa Rica, right here, right now, get birds close up, full color? The whole thing, all you want." He turned again to the computer, his hands were on the keyboard.

"No, please," Rufus said, "don't spoil it for me. I want those birds in the flesh and feathers, close up or not."

"Okay, gotcha." He smiled. "That's *your* explorer thing."

"I suppose it is. Okay, as long as you're dying to bring up something from that machine, how many panthers in Florida?"

"This is like an exam?"

"I'm a numbers man, that's all. I'd like a figure, an estimate. Florida panthers are on the verge of extinction."

Charlie was already at work, his hands busy, brightly colored windows came and went, Rufus recognizing only two of them: Center for Biological Diversity and U.S. Fish and Wildlife Service.

"Here," Charlie said, "state-by-state stats. Now we click on Florida. Panther. *Felis concolor*. That it?"

"That's it."

Charlie began mumbling to himself as he read the biology, range, status etc. "Here we go, latest estimate: one hundred and sixty. But there's another estimate: Less than a hundred. They don't really know."

"Not knowing is a big player in this game"

"Endangered species game." Charlie sat back, looking thoughtful.

Rufus said, "Yes, I suppose it is sort of game. Never thought of it like that. Well, I'd best be going." He rose slowly from the chair and rubbed his hip. "I've taken up enough of your time. Good luck on that book report."

Charlie came back from whatever he'd been thinking. "There's a tiger in the book."

"You mentioned that."

"Pi, that's the boy on the raft. Oh and that's a math symbol, right? Anyway, Pi, he's getting to know the tiger's habits, he's scared of it, but sometimes feels sort of friendly, but I think maybe the tiger doesn't give a damn about Pi."

"Makes you wonder, doesn't it, about cats."

"The tiger's a cat, that's right. A humongous cat."

"Endangered too, just like those Florida cats." He walked stiffly to the foot of the stairs.

Charlie stood and called out. "Where's your next stop?"

"Home, day's drive from here, check up on my cat."

Wayne, bowing against a relentless wind, rode south-east then east on I-80, reaching Laramie well before noon. He stopped at a Mini-Mart, inquired about the address Jennifer had given him. No problem, the house was on a tree-shaded block near the university. Wayne propped the bike and crossed a small, drouth-scorched lawn to the door, knocked and waited, nervously.

A woman opened the door. She was barefooted, wearing jeans and a short-sleeved shirt with a message in black letters. WILDERNESS WATCH. Her face was weathered. Dark eyes, black hair cut short.

Wayne asked if she was Cerise Santmeyer.

"Cerise is at work and I"m about to leave."

"Right, uh, sorry to bother you. It's about Breakout."

"We're not in that any more. We've got enough trouble." Her voice rose, "Leave us alone, you hear?"

"Damn those Feds," Wayne said, and backed away from her. "Look, don't panic, I'll leave you alone. I'm working for Breakout, got an assignment, you might say" He grinned. "Orders from headquarters, up at Rock River. You know Rock River?"

She was staring at him. He went on. "I'm supposed to contact a few people who've been bothered by the Feds. Talk, that's all."

She noticed his bike. "That Harley's yours?"

He turned. "Yeah. Gave it an overhawl down in Arizona. It's humming good now. You're a biker?"

"My partner and I ride a lot on weekends. Went up Steamboat Mountain once, in the Red Desert."

"I know that mountain. Lately I've been really eatin' up the country, Endangered Species work." He laughed and took another backward step. "I don't know much about it, actually. Trying to learn."

"I suppose I could meet you someplace. Not here. I go to work at one."

"How about Applebee's? My treat."

They got in ahead of the noon crowd, took the booth next to the door, asked for coffee. "I'm Jeanne," she said, "hardly ever eat here. Cerise and I are on a tight budget."

"Me too, up to now, but just the other day Breakout put me on salary. I'm Wayne Callahan." He held out his hand. She took it. "You've got ingrained grease," she said, and smiled. The coffee came, they ordered.

Jeanne said, "Cerise is the one you were supposed to talk to." She looked at the display of photos on the wall. Folk singers, cowboys, sirens: Western eclectic.

"Cerise and I, we're partners."

"Okay. You work outdoors a lot.".

"I guess it shows. Sun and wind. Maintenance crew, at the U. And Cerise...you don't have to know.

"No, 'course not."

"It's not easy, Cerise and me. This is Wyoming, you know."

"Sure."

"Where you from?"

He sketched his recent life. Family breakup, left wife and two boys in Great Falls, Montana, biked south, met Rufus Knutson, birdwatcer. As soon as he began the somewhat humorous story of how he'd met Rufus, he faltered. "Complicated."

She sighed, but with a slight smile. "I know about complicated. Stuff that might harm someody else."

"You guessed it, but I can talk about Breakout."

To: BREAKOUT@LISTSERV.SPEAKUP.ORG

From: gballard@earthlink.com

Re: Feds

Security people, a man and a woman, came to where I work, last Friday, asked questions about Breakout and me and my family. I have a big family, kids, grandkids, cousins. Will I post any more on Breakout? On any other list? Don't know. Honestly, I just don't know.

gilbert

Wayne returned to I-80, went west to Wyoming 789 and then south. Low hills and raggedy sagebrush plains. Muddy Creek received Cow Creek from the east and shortly thereafter, Wild Cow Creek. Wayne liked it all, remembering grand spreads of land in Montana, rough terrain with gullies that led into faraway heights. He came to Baggs, topped off the bike's tank and bought a root beer.

On into Colorado. At Craig he asked for the turn-off for the Crow Bar. He found it, a gravelled road that soon turned to dirt as it wound through a shallow valley. Dense groves of willows, magpies in attendance. The ranch entrance was a pine pole cattle guard. The Crow Bar's brand was burned into a slab of wood that was nailed onto a barbed wire fence post. Wayne cut the ignition and silence swept in. No, there was a faint sound. It had Wayne stumped for a moment, then he got it, the thump of hay bales thrown from a truck bed. He smiled, remembering the season he'd bucked bales on the Iverson place north of Rose Hill.

He rode across a slight rise to a view of ranch headquarters. Pole barn, frame house with generous screened veranda, aluminum roofed hay barn, corral, tractor shed. The action was at the hay shed, two men unloading a truck. They glanced at Wayne, but kept the work going. Wayne glided to the truck, stopped, parked the bike and helmet. "I'd really and truly like to spell somebody," he said.

The man on he ground plunked a bale into place at the base of a high stack that nearly filled the shed. He spoke to a much younger man on the truck bed. "Step down, Jimmy, let the man pitch in."

Jimmy grinned down at Wayne, collected both hay hooks in his left hand and jumped off the truck. He offered the hooks to Wayne.

"Thanks, man," Wayne said, happy as a lark. The gift of labor.

Jimmy went into the house, saying he'd heat up the coffee, but the man in the shed called out. "Throw that old stuff out, make new."

They finished the job in no time. "That's the last load, by god and it better last us through the winter, the cost of this stuff you wouldn't believe. You from Breakout?"

"Yes. Wayne Callahan."

"Clarence Lomax."

They shook hands and headed for the house. Clarence said, "I assume you're here to give me some counsel."

"Hell no, I'm here to listen and talk."

A dog lay panting in house shade. Jimmy was in the veranda pouring coffee. Clarence said, "It's not that we're worried, Jimmy and me, just curious, can't figure out why this pair of homeland security guys would come way out here to the Crow Bar. You'd think they'd have more important things to do. And so do we, that's for sure. Jimmy and I've got more than we can handle, trying to hang onto the ranch. My wife passed, last winter; we're trying to get over that; well, it's not something you get over. So, when these two federals drove in here we were not in a good mood. Tell you the truth, we were downright hostile." He smiled, looking at his boots. "Happened we had hay hooks in our hands at the time, just like when you arrived here today. The feds looked a mite nervous, turned on the charm full bore. My god, Wayne, you should've seen them two, so damn respectful you couldn't believe a word they said, and all decked out in long ties and pressed pants."

They reached the screen door of the veranda and Clarence held it open for Wayne. Jimmy had put three cups on a small ranch-made table and was drawing up chairs. They sat down. Wayne asked, "What was their line?"

"Giving us a heads up. This Breakout outfit might be a front for terrorists."

"Environmental variety."

"No. You'd expect that, wouldn't you. No, just plain *terrorists*."

Jimmy said, "Dad's on a list, that's what it's all about." He was teasing and it was an old story and his dad said, wearily,, "Shot an antelope out of season, big deal. Besides, it was state game warden, not federal."

"Antelope, best eating there is," Wayne said, winking at Jimmy.

"Getting arrested does start you going over all the crazy things you've done," Clarence said, "but we're pretty damn ordinary."

Wayne drank some coffee. "Thanks, Jimmy, this is just what the doctor ordered. You know, my guess is the federals by now has got just about the whole population listed."

"I don't see how that makes their job any easier," Clarence said.

"Spread nervousness around," Jimmy said.

Clarence nodded. "They did a pretty good job of it around here. There's this rancher over on Sand Creek, wife recently ran out on him. He goes around telling his sorrow, people getting a little fed up with that. Well, he gets wind of these two agents dropping in on Jimmy and me and he starts speculating and it's not long before he's got a story, how we're linked into some conspiracy or other. Didn't make sense, but these days nothing makes sense anyway so people listened to him and they start speculating too and on and on it goes."

"Dad, nobody took it as gospel truth."

"No, and they know old Frances, know he's the county's first class gossip, but you got to remember, Jimmy, tucked away in back of everybody's mind is this story about us here at the Crow Bar. It's there, people don't mean us no harm, but it's there, tucked away, waiting its chance."

"Yeah Dad, but you and me told the real story; what the agents said, what we said, the whole nine yards of the whole damn episode."

"Well yes, there's that. And what we said about Breakout. We stuck up for it."

Wayne looked at each of them in turn. "You did?"

Clarence shook his head yes, remembering. "We did. We'd been reading some of the things people were putting on that e-mail thing."

"Listserv," Jimmy said.

"Whatever. Well, we took an interest, all these different ideas, some we'd thought of ourselves. Land and animals, just talk, back and forth. Wasn't all decked out with buttons to push to get more blah-blah from some expert who's written books and gets free rein to tell all of us the score like on some dumbass interview program on the TV. So yes, Wayne, be assured, we did stick up for Breakout. Say, why don't you stay the night?" He stood up. "Right now we've got chores to do."

Wayne said, "I'll take you up on that. Cut me in on the chores."

Clarence led the way into the warm, sage- and aspen- and balsam root-scented early evening.

After supper...steak and potatoes and store-bought pie...they sat up late, Clarence the most talkative but Jimmy getting in his sly bits, and Wayne storing things for future thought on the long and lonesome tour of the universe. How good it was to have company, to sit back, legs outstretched, taking it all in, the shadings of voices, the darkness, the whispering of night, and once the faint yip-yip of a coyote.

By the time Jimmy had piled the dishes in the sink his dad was repeating himself, but with added vehemence. "You take that Zapus woman up in Chugwaer, asks who owns Wyoming? Well, she knows the answer to that as well as any of us. The question she's asking there is, you see, a part of her sticking up for that little mouse."

"She's okay, Dad," Jimmy said.

"Didn't say she wasn't. I've nothing against the mouse and I'm the first to say we've got some real strange old geezers amongst us cow people who are bound and determined to go against every damned thing the government does, if it takes every horse in the barn."

"Not just cow people, Dad. Sheep people, don't leave them out."

"All right, all right. The main thing is, the most of us are in the job of trying to make ends meet. Is there some law against that?"

Wayne asked, "What kind of mouse is this, up in Chugwater?"

Clarence and Jimmy gave him a surprised look. Clarence said, "Jumping mouse, endangered species, or species of special concern, or threatened, they keep changing their minds about it."

"Scientific name is Zapus," Jimmy said. "We're supposed to have some in Colorado too. I think I might've seen one once."

"I'm surprised at you, Wayne. Don't you read the stuff on Breakout?"

"Posts, Dad, not stuff."

Wayne said, "I've been on the road almost all the time Breakout's been around. Had a few days off and they went and put me on the board and then I hit the road again."

"You're on the Breakout Board?" Jimmy asked.

"Yeah, but it's Jennifer and Enid who do the real work."

"That Enid, she's smart," Clarence said. "She's the one wrote that bit about the feds and how Breakout is all about people talking, not about terrorism."

"Free speech place," Jimmy said;.

"You guys are way ahead of me," Wayne said. "Looks like I better catch up on my reading."

"What I was trying to get to, about that Zapus woman," Clarence resumed, "she's like a lot of others speaking on Breakout, sticking up for one animal, getting all excited about that one, like that guy down in Texas…"

"Jason," Jimmy said. "Austin, Texas."

"Right. He's all for the toad, which is fine with me; I've got nothing against toads; more of them the better, but what I'm saying is, people like that don't listen to people who're trying to make a living."

"People on the land," Jimmy added.

Clarence tilted his chair back, put his hands behind his head. "A person gets worked up, you know?"

"I know," Wayne said.

Clarence was on a roll. "Those environmentalists, think they're the ones to decide everything for everybody. A lot of them are plumb loco about cows. Cows are not native, they come from

Europe, so they've got to be bad, out there eating and shitting and hanging around water. Well, sweet Jesus, is that any reason to hate cows? Angus, Hereford, Longhorn, Charolais, Shorthorn, whatever, those animals love swamps and shallow creeks; they have a strong hankering to put their hooves in mud and stand there and eat and drink and soak up a good living. Well, it's their nature, dammit. What are cows supposed to do, go off and shoot theirselves?"

Jimmy said, "So then the enviros ask why can't you stingy ranchers hire a herd of cowboys to keep cows away from *riparian areas*."

Clarence tipped his head toward Jimmy, winked at Wayne. "A year at cow college."

"Not a cow college, Dad. They changed the name, it's a university."

"This Zapus woman," Wayne asked, "she's one who hates cows?"

"Well, no, I don't get that impression," Clarence said. "What do you think, Jimmy?

"She talks to ranchers, Dad. I'll give her that."

"I'll be heading back to Wyoming," Wayne said. "Maybe I'll look her up."

To: BREAKOUT@LISTSERV.SPEAKUP.ORG

From: todda@frontiernet.net

Re: Federals

Had a couple FBIs knock on our door a few days ago. We could see they wanted some dirt on Breakout, but we didn't have any. Their story was that we activists need to be aware that environmentalism is one of those "segments of society" that are possible sources of terrorist "intrusion." And so on, like that.

When they left Lou and I sat down for some serious discussion. We decided to give ourselves some peace of mind. We realized it's only a relative peace, but relative is all we can reach for in these times. We gave ourselves an answer to this question: Give in or gear up? We decided to gear up.

So, to all of you out there, Peace. Remember, it's a matter of who's to be master, Them or Us. We choose Us.

Todd and Lou

To the Editor

Casper Star Tribune

I want to reply to people who have, in this paper, and on the street too, jumped all over me for defending jumping mice.

I took every chance I got to ask local ranchers how they felt about the mouse. The results are interesting. One ranch woman didn't know what I was talking about. I explained that the federal Fish and Wildlife Service had located areas in Platte county and other places as "areas of concern" for protection of *Zapus*, the jumping mouse. She said she was sick and tired of government trying to tell us what to do and not do. I said there might be, once in a while, a government action that's more good than bad. She thought that might be possible.

Another rancher said he'd mow hay damn well where he pleased, but after we got to talking more about it I got the impression he was not mad at the mouse, he was mad at government.

Another rancher told me he knew all about Zapus and compared to the hell of coalbed methane drillers he didn't see that this little creature was all that big a problem.

Another rancher said that some of the things environmentalists said made sense, and some were just plain arrogant know-it-alls. So, I asked, what can be done about that? And we had quite an interesting talk, mainly about who owns Wyoming. I was the one brought that up.

I hope I've quoted these people correctly. I grew up on a ranch, by the way, though I've been a townie for a long time.

Very truly yours,

Anna Browning

Enid walked from her house to the highway to stop in the sparse shade of the cottonwood that spread itself against the sunburned false-fronted building, survivor from the days of cattle drives, uranium strikes, hopes of hefty tourist travel. Enid knew a little Rock River history now, having hobnobbed with its citizens, though she was often surprised by how recently some of those citizens had arrived, from California, middle west, rmountain west, east.

She had come to realize that she was living in a huge transition time. But maybe the west had always been in transition. The Old West of mining, ranching, lumbering and farming was fading, or so everyone said, giving way to the New West, the amenities culture. Living in Rock River for the few weeks of her new life, her Breakout life, Enid hoped that the New West picture was wrong, that it wouldn't ripen. She sensed that neither of the wests were truly attentive to the land and the animals and the people. She hoped that there was another west, scattered, hidden, out-gunned, but there.

A mild wind began to ruffle the heat. Cotton-wood leaves made their soothing sounds. Enid went back to her house. The phone was ringing. She hurried inside, snatched up the phone, hoping it was Rufus. Wayne had reported; Rufus, as always, was late.

"Is this Breakout?"

"Yes, Enid Shaw speaking."

"I'm calling from Lemmon, South Dakota, about stopping war."

"Lemmon?"

"Near Grand river, next to North Dakota border. We were hoping you species people might be interested."

"I see, well, as you know, our interest is pretty much taken up with the extinction crisis."

"War has to do with that. War has a lot to do with everything. Three of us here in Lemmon are calling everyone who is possibly wanting to quit trying to run the world by force and use our national treasury for things that need doing

We decided to stop war. One of us was a nurse in Vietnam and another lost a husband in, well, what do you know, I forget which war. She owns The Hair Affair. And me, I'm Terrie McKenna, presently living in one of these assisted living places."

Enid sat down, her thoughts in a whirl, torn between hanging up on a fanatic and wanting to hear more of the amazing certainty in the woman's voice. "Tell me more," she said.

"Sharon Sanchez, she mans the desk at Alex Lee's garage, and Gretchen Hoffman, she has *The Hair Affair*. We will go to where State Route 73 meets U.S. 12. I think our signs will say, BRING EVERYBODY HOME. Or maybe REGIME CHANGE BEGINS AT HOME.

"Only you three?"

"Oh my goodness no, we're scaring up more folks. Right now we're putting out invitations to all sorts of organizations to join us."

"At Lemmon?"

"Oh no." Again her laugh, thin, raspy. "Across the whole damn country, sea to shining sea."

Enid visualized the woman: slight, but not lean? Earrings? Hair in some sort of wave, created at *The Hair Affair*? She said, "I'm willing to think about this."

"Go ahead, but don't take too long. We're inviting everybody to make a sign, whatever they want to say, and take that sign and go to a highway junction. Like, there's an Isaac Walton League chapter in Rapid City. They deal with species, by the way. Some of them, unofficially, promise to stand at U.S. 126 and I-90. And we've contacted people on Standing Rock Reservation; some of them are interested. We'll organize South Dakota, don't you worry about that."

"That's the program? Stand at junctions?"

"Yes, We figured that drivers have to slow down at junctions, sometimes stop; gives them a chance to see what's going on. Probably a Saturday, real soon. The idea is, whoever's president will need to hear from citizens."

"That's been tried, more than once."

"No, you're wrong there, Honey. This will be coast-to-coast; won't be just a million people who can afford two or three days to go to Washington or San Francisco to make big crowds and listen to a bunch of celebrities talk way too long and then drag home dog tired and hope the TV will show a minute or two of the big crowd, and the TV will downplay it, we all know that, and then everybody gets sad and that's the end of it and whatever war we're in goes on. So, you see, this showing is not for military experts, like retired generals and professors and spin doctors from government. It's not for renowned liberals or heads of this and that. It's for all of us, for whoever gets out there and stands proud. No podium, no loudspeakers, just people on the roads, on a certain day, at a certain two or three hours."

"Interesting," Enid said, "but doesn't it risk harrassment? One person at a junction, or just a few, all alone?"

"Hey, you want everything peaches and cream? This action is what we call a showing. People showing to people, and it will be hard to think up an excuse for not choosing a place nearby and then go there. You understand me?"

"I can't speak for the people who are active on the Breakout listserv or who visit our web site."

"No, course not, but you could get with a few people and organize Wyoming."

"What?"

"Somebody's got to do it. Wyoming only has about half a million people, last I heard. Look, I gotta go, I'm half way down this long list of places to call. We each of us have a list, but people keep coming up with more addresses to add to the lists and I've started telling them thank you very much, call them yourself. Some of them do."

"Can I call you back?"

"No. This line will be busy. I'll send you my e-mail address, to remind you. Now get cracking, woman, make yourself a nice sandwich and sit down and think."

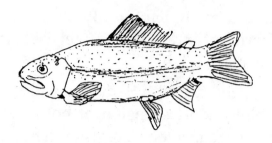

Cedar Walk Lodge, New Hampshire.

Once a lively horse-and-buggy resort, still lively, and decorous. Helen Smithson, alone on a comfortable chair on the veranda that overlooked the lake and served as a bright adjunct to the dining room. She watched the manager make his leisurely way from guest to guest. She admired his spontaneity, quick laughter, attentive manner. She wondered what he would say to her, and how she might respond? Such an idle thought. Is this the trivial finish of this life journey?

At the other end of the veranda, Sam and Paul. Helen knew what they were having for breakfast; Sam's would be bacon, eggs over easy and toast; Paul would ever so precisely cut French toast into little squares. No problem with that, in ordinary circumstances, but Helen and Paul and Sam had created a circumstance not so ordinary.

It had begun with Paul calling Sam "the valiant activist," at first in friendly jest. Helen had joined the back-and-forth banter. By the time they entered Vermont and found a motel the tease had taken on a sharp edge.

However, the tiff with Sam was endurable. It was the blind condescension of both Sam and Paul that enraged Helen. A registered nurse with a long career of taking charge of tough situations, she felt herself demoted to passive victim of a disregard excruciatingly entwined in an utterly unconscious Victorian politeness in every relation that included her. And the two men monopolized the front of the SUV, trading off on the driving, both of them reckless and inattentive. Helen sat in back, fuming, certain that they would never reach New Hampshire and Cedar Walk Lodge, venue of the Third Annual Meeting of the Ecological Ethics Society.

Sam's idea: crash the meeting, find a strategically key place in the proceedings whereupon Sam would rise up to denounce the arrogant complacency of the distinguished gathering situated in an omnipresent world where thousands of species slide into oblivion while war and reckless greed among humans blocks action and takes monstrous toll.

Helen had gone along with the plan. The idea of speaking out loud in flaming rhetoric had for her a strong appeal. But that wasn't why she had teamed up with the two men; she had wanted out of Harbor View, desperately; opportunity arriving, she had grabbed it.

Now, watching Sam and Paul amiably chatting, she asked herself if they weren't as totally unaware of "the omnipresent world" as any of the complacent academics, many of whom were there in plain sight, breakfasting jovially, pointedly paying no attention to Sam and Paul and the woman who, yesterday, had stood loyally with them.

The manager approached. Fortyish, round-faced, lips pursed, altogether pleasant. "You are alone today," he said.

That provoked Helen. "Well, aren't you the observant one."

"My apology, please, I don't mean to pry, but stories about you and your two companions are everywhere."

'I suppose they are. We certainly did make fools of ourselves."

"Ah, but so do others. Conferences, we have hosted so many here, so many important people from the higher echelons."

"I had this illusion," she said. suddenly feeling an overwhelming need to speak and reveal, "that ecologists, dealing with the very roots of the organization of life would somehow be less conventional."

"Ah, perhaps not so. May I sit down? " Not waiting for her permission, he sat. "I am conventional too, but at times one enjoys plain speaking. That was what happened yesterday, so I'm told. Your friends spoke to me."

"Not exactly friends, more like temporary fellow travelers. The three of us are, as you see, old people. Sam in his seventies with the emotions of a young man who has discovered the Holy Grail."

"Sam? The one who spoke yesterday?"

"Yes."

"But I, hearing of his, ah, what was referred to as 'a performance,' I was pleased."

"I'm glad someone appreciated it."

"I dare to suggest you take it too seriously. Upscale persons deserve an occasional drenching with cold water."

"Not that it improves them."

"No." He leaned forward and spoke softly. "It is for the benefit of us who live on somewhat lower slopes. Our amusement, you see?"

"I'll try to look at it that way,"

He said, "I am Quebecoise, from Montreal, At one time a chef. I am Maurice."

"Helen. A registered nurse. Suddenly found myself relegated to a nursing home. I walked out, in company with those two men. Foolish, but I'm glad I did it."

Maurice took the time to consider what she had just said. She appreciated that. When he asked her where next she and her companions might go she said she had no idea. He stood and told her he was pleased to have made her acquantance and she believed him. "The pleasure is all mine, Maurice. I wonder, do you suppose I might find access to a computer, only for the purpose of sending an e-mail?"

"I am sorry," he said, "we have no cyber cafe, but I would be happy to lead you to the office where we have network access. My own computer, you are welcome to use it."

"Wonderful. One short e-mail, that's all I require, quite urgently."

To: eshaw@wyoming.com

From: helsmith@earthlink.com

Re: Harbor View fugitives

Dear Enid Shaw, I write to you backchannel regarding three ill fated old crocks from Harbor View. Your funds supported us this far, but we have no useful plans for paying you back in good works. I have to be honest. First, I know only generalities about ecology and endangered species. Second, I have fallen out with my companions, two tunnel visioned males from the Pleistocene.

My request: Can you order us to do something actually useful, something that won't simply endorse the wild tactics of an over-the-top environmental activist?

Disclosure: I have a heart pacer, but can walk without falling. Former RN, I require little medical advice. That is not as arrogant as it sounds. I can recognize an emergency in my own internal workings, in which case I seek help. Otherwise, I am fiercely independent. I insist on full equality, especially when it comes to making decisions that affect all of any group. I hope that what was done here at Cedar Walk did at least show to a gathering of academics that Breakout exists.

Please help me! If you reply it will be to the above address, which is not mine. It belongs to the manager of Cedar Walk Lodge. If he happens to read our correspondence that is fine with me. He has been kind and understanding.

Helen Smithson

To: mlaurier@earthlink.com

From: eshaw@wyoming.com

Re: Harbor View fugitives

Dear Helen, We strongly suggest you three go to Grayling, Michigan where we have accomodations for you at Quiet Pines Motel.

En route please stop in Malone, New York state, and contact David Corwin: High Trails Assisted Living Unit, 879 Cottonwood.

Dave and several others there are creating an issue of what Breakout people refer to as "species singles," a heavy weight sheet of paper that presents basic data on a species or group of species. The Malone production is quite ambitious: commercial fisheries off the northeast coast. I understand it features a barn door skate swimming across the top. A run of 1,000 should be coming off the press in Malone any day, destined for the Quebec/New York border area. Wait for that. If at all possisble contribute your own energies to the door-to-door work of distribution of these sheets.

FYI, another species single is underway in Laramie, Wyoming, featuring Wyoming toads and that is to be followed by an issue on sage grouse. Exciting things happening all across the country. You can catch up on all that at Quiet Pines and become acquainted with the travelers from Maple View, and make plans.

I don't like to think of you and Sam and Paul all by yourselves and out of contact. I take special notice of your insistence on equality.

Enid

U.S. 20, Nebraska.

Sunset light gleaming, heavy rain with an interval of hail had passed. Thunder still growled in the east. Howie Blake's '97 GMC pickup rumbled along as good as could be expected. Howie was tired and he was late, but now at last Chadron welcomed him with a battered banner, blue letters on white cloth.

SHARP-TAIL DAY.

He found the left turn to the high school, drove along a pleasant street shaded by trees on one side, playing fields on the other. He yawned, began circling the gym, found the loading dock, backed in, put the brake on, yawned again and got out. He banged on the metal door and waited. Hearing voices inside, he banged again and stepped back. The door opened. Two husky and weathered men stood there in shirtsleeves, baggy pants, comical hats made of stiff paper shaped to resemble a bird's head.

Howie grinned. "Sharp-tail grouse?"

The two men laughed and pointed at each other. "I'm George," one of them said, "and this is Dennis. You're the piano man."

"At your service." They shook hands.

Dennis said. "We're having a little trouble with the mikes."

Howie looked inside. "I like the lighting."

"Subdued like," George said, "that was Maureen's idea. She's the one in charge."

Howie walked in, presented himself to the woman crouched at the sound board. Black skirt, white blouse, hair tied back by a narrow blue ribbon, tiny turquoise earrings. She got up, looked him over. "You are, I trust, the piano man."

"Howie."

"Hello, Howie, I'm Maureen." She was distraught, but that didn't keep her from giving him a close examination, making him aware of his travel-worn jeans and unfestive shirt.

"We open in twenty minutes, lots of people here, waiting, makes me nervous."

Howie said, "Do without the mikes, if we have to."

"Well, there's an idea, the first good one I've heard in some time." She glanced accusingly at

George and Dennis, who grinned back at her. Suddenly, Maureen laughed. "Oh you goddamn musicians, I suppose this is all old hat to you. Make do and get on with the show."

"As for us being musicians, we're strictly boondocks level," Dennis said.

Shaking his head, chuckling, Howie said, "No, we're music makers and we're here to put on a damn good show. Who's the caller?"

"Dennis," George said, "and he's good."

Maureen went back to being worried. "This dance has to go over big. I want people to remember sharp-tail grouse and I want those memories to be good ones."

Dennis and George looked a little like scolded schoolboys, but Howie said, "Yes, Ma'am, we'll do you proud. The piano's out in my truck."

People were still wandering in, looking around, impatient. A king-size sheet was tethered at the far end of the gym, below the basketball net. Some talented person had painted two male sharp-tailed grouse in mating stomp mode and a female grouse looking them over. At their feet black letters.

THEY NEED HABITAT

Howie stepped to one of three mikes. "Can you hear me? You, way back there, speak up."

Someone yelled, "Yes, but it's rough."

Howie went to the sound board, studied it, made an adjustment, nodded to Maureen who tried the mike again.

From the floor another yell. "That's better, let's get the show on the road."

Howie stepped to the mike. "We need a couple husky lads or maids up here to wrassle the piano."

Half a dozen people hustled to the stage. Babs and Sylvie were at the entrance, handing out sea turtle singles. Voices, footsteps, echoes. Howie felt his feet tingle. It was always this way, tiredness gone lurking somewhere, the long highway drag forgotten.

Dennis came up to him, tuning his guitar. "Sorry we couldn't fit in a spot of practice."

"My fault, got a late start, ran into some weather. I'll just tag along with you guys for awhile."

"Usually I don't worry, but that Maureen, she's set her whole heart and soul into this festival. The parade went pretty well, people took it okay. You know, tolerant, fair amount of excitement. But she's like running full-tilt, wants the whole herd in the pasture bellowing joy. Know what I mean? Makes me kinda worried."

"Well, let's do it. By the way, I'd better tell you, I'm not really an environmentalist. Was surfing web pages the other day, happened upon Break-out. Some of the thoughts struck me about right, but I'm more into the idea of saving people. Like, 'Iraqis are people,' that kind of thing."

"I don't have any problem with that."

George, at one of the mikes, stage whispered to Dennis and Howie. "Folks are gettin' jumpy."

Dennis swaggered to the center mike, making the most of his broad shoulders and massive chest. "You gettin' restless, George? Uh huh, I see he is. Look at the man, got fire in his eye."

George brought his bow down on the strings, hard and clangy and did a bit of foot shuffle.

"George is rarin' to go, we can't delay any longer." Dennis struck a cord. "Find yourself a partner and take hands in one big circle. Quick step now, the tide's in."

He watched the circle form. "This will be a warm-up. If you don't know all the moves don't fret, loosen up and somebody will shove you around. Are you all holding hands? George here is on the fiddle and Howie's on the ivories and me with this old git tar, we're steppin' out tonight, a fine prairie evening in Nebraska, a great prairie state, a proud state, a wonderful place to drum our feet on the good earth."

Scattered applause.

"I want you all to circle to the left and we'll wing it from there. His guitar spoke, George's fiddle squealed, the piano came in with a strong background beat.

"Now circle left, tap your feet,
this is the place where the sharp-tails meet
.................turn about and circle right
Smile at your partner, smile............
Bow to your partner, bow...............
Swing your partner, swing...............
doh-see-doh your partner now
shake them feathers, you know how
doh-see-doh your neighbor.........listen
for my call..........
Allemande left with your left hand,
right to your partner and a right and left grand
.... lift those shanks.........stomp the earth
raise some dust...................
watch for your partner, watch.

....

There she is and every body swing
one and two and three and four
............lead your honeybunch
off the floor and you know where
and I don't care."

Maureen, standing among the scattered few who were not dancing, clapped her hands softly. She looked around for someone with whom she might share her delight. Otis. She went to him. "I can't thank you enough, for bringing all this to poor old Chadron."

"It's our pleasure. Chadron's a nice town."

"Long way from Michigan. You must be tired."

Though that was true, Otis protested. "We're fine."

Dennis began to urge people onto the floor again, five or six couples for each set. Otis noticed Maureeen giving him an openly speculative look. She made her move. "Shall we?"

He began to protest, but was suddenly struck by the thought that of all the ways to die, this one ranked pretty high on the desirability scale. He allowed Maureen to take his arm in a strong grip and lead him to the nearest set. Babs, hawk-eyed, mimed to Sylvie. "Do you see what I see?"

Sylvie searched until she spotted Otis and Maureen. She giggled in anticipation.

At the piano the musicians conferred, Howie tapped out a few bars of *Soldier's Joy*. Dennis and George chimed in. George nodded, Dennis wasn't quite satisfied. Howie tried *Redwing* and fiddle, guitar and piano swung into it with a delicate abandon. They were ready.

Maureen, tuned to a high pitch, tried to catch the crowd's mood. Was the dance going to be all right? Or, maybe, stupendous? She wasn't sure; she wasn't paying much attention to Otis who stood quietly at her side, happy and relaxed beyond any mood he could have imagined a few minutes ago.

Babs whispered to Sylvie, "Otis looks good."

Dennis shouted "You did well, folks, now let's form sets, circle up four."

Confusion on the floor, but Dennis stood back from the mike, watched those who understood his demands take charge. A good enough order soon prevailed. Dennis strummed a chord. "Listen to my call folks, you'll catch on soon enough. Further along we have a figure that can be a mite difficult. Ah, Maureen and the gentleman with you, and your neighbor couple, could you four demonstrate? Thank you. No music, just walk it through."

Otis, now happily accepting disaster, felt Maureen's left hand in his right and his neighbor's right took his left. At the doorway Sylvie murmured to Babs, "Dennis, that rascal, setting them up on purpose."

Maud sidled over to them."Do you see what I see?"

Dennis called. "Circle four…………Good, good, hold that, don't break it up…here we go, dive for the oyster."

Maureen led Otis into a dive between their neighbors. Otis tried to go all the way. "Stop," Maureen hissed, "back out."

He obeyed.

Dennis called, "Dive for the clam."

Maureen held Otis firmly in place while the opposite couple did the diving.

"Piece of cake," Otis whispered.

"Just wait," Maureen said.

"Now take the whole damn can."

Otis, in a fortunate flash of insight, guessed what was coming and the opposite partners knew too and the four of them did the entire inside out, twisting like trout through a sluice and came out smiling.

Dennis, grinning like a Cheshire cat, shouted praise. "Beautiful. All foursomes will be doing that. Ready? I'll be throwing in some doh-see-dohs and one thing and another. Listen for my call."

Maureen whispered to Otis, "It's easier with music."

Dennis was doing his loose-knees bounce. He was a good caller because he had an easy-going patter and sensitive timing and a firm knowledge of all the figures, but also because it was great fun.

"Enough love-making," he shouted, "let's have music."

To: BREAKOUT@LISTSERV.SPEAKUP.ORG

From: hsand@northstar.net

Re: Wolf

I live in Minnesota, west of Rainy Lake, been interested in /Canis lupus/ all my life

It's said that wolves kill or chase coyotes out of their territories. This means fewer coyotes to prey on other animals like mice, gophers, squirrels, rabbits. The result, in theory, is a bigger share of prey for hawks, owls, eagles, foxes, minks, etc.

Wolves normally go after big animals like moose, elk, cattle. When they make a kill they feast; when they go away, even a small distance, ravens, magpies, foxes, coyotes and others move in for clean-up. Having wolves around changes things.

However, biologists I've been talking to keep warning me that we don't know everything. For example, by killing elk do the wolves reduce elk numbers enough to insure elk food stays plentiful and of good quality? Food quality for elk, deer, mountain sheep and other herbivores is important. Those animals need decent food just like we do. Just any old stuff growing in drouth conditions or depleted soil won't do.

Another point: conditions are bound to be different in Wyoming and Montana, compared to Minnesota, New Mexico, Alaska, Quebec.

Chadron, Nebraska.

Morning after the sharp-tail dance. Maureen, excited and hopeful, went to the motel where the Breakout crew was housed. She caught sight of Otis and Maud and Herb moving slowly down the street, looking for a late breakfast. She trotted across the street. "I have news. Valentine heard about the festival. Front page story."

"Who's Valentine?" Herb asked.

"It's a town, east of here. A friend of mine just now called me up, asked if they could have you there for a concert or dance, whatever you would like to put on."

"Valentine, I love you," Maud said, "but right now I'm looking for my coffee fix."

"I simply had to let you know."

Otis said, "The festival was on the front page?"

"Yes, and especially the dance."

"We'll get together, decide."

"I know it's a lot to ask," she said. "I mean, after all …"

"Yes," Maud said, "we're old and frail. Not much can be expected of us."

"I didn't…well, yes, I did, to some degree, not exactly the way you …. Oh, I'm confused."

Maud was laughing. "No, you're right on."

To: BREAKOUT@LISTSERV.SPEAKUP.ORG

From: jennf@wyoming.com

Re: Ferrets

I work at a place where ferrets are raised in captivity for eventual release in the wild. Many of the releases have not been successful. Predators, such as coyotes, take a toll. And disease. And there is a serius shortage of large prairie dog colonies.

Recently a new finding suggests something hopeful.

In a cave in White Pine Mountains, Nevada a skull of a black-footed ferret, /Mustela nigripes/, was discovered and analyzed carefully to make sure it wasn't a mink or any other member of the mustelid tribe (sea otters, weasels etc.). The age of the skull was determined to be at least 750,000 years. In the same level of debris in that cave were positively identified skeletal remains of ground squirrels, pack rats, rabbits, deer mice and field mice, but no prairie dogs. Other places where ancient bones of black-footed ferrets have been found (ranging from Texas to Yukon Territory) were similar: no prairie dog remains.

These findings suggest that ferrets living 750,000 years ago did not prey on prairie dogs. That dependence must have come later, in "modern" times. Is it possible that our captive ferrets here at Sybille and other places could be trained to capture ground squirrels and mice, in additon to, or even instead of, prairie dogs? Jennifer

Valentine, Nebraska.

The Breakout travelers, arriving early, found enough vacancies at Motel Downtown to house all of them. Herb and Otis, lugging their meagre belongings into one of the doubles, wasted no time in stretching themselves out on the beds. Otis, feeling mischievous, challenged Herb to come up with the latest data on whitebark pine.

Herb refused the bait. "You know damn well I don't know a thing about those pines, other than they're having a hard time of it."

Otis said. "High altitude tree, very similar to limber pine."

"Oh sure, you know something about everything."

"Herb, neither one of us could pass an exam on pines."

They were silent for a few moments, staring at the ceiling. Otis said, "This that we're doing now, beats Maple View life."

"I have to agree," Herb said.

They fell asleep.

Motel Downtown had a flagstone patio supplied with an abundance of white plastic armchairs and shaded by black locust and russian olive. The travelers found it, one by one, near suppertime. Conversation was languid with big gaps, the heat oppressive. Maureen appeared, with ice tea and plastic cups. Leonard helped her pour and serve. Herb rattled the ice in his tea. "This is the life."

"We pay for it," George said. "I mean not just Breakout money. Blood, our own, if you don't mind my saying so."

"I don't mind. Interesting work, you meet all kinds."

"Some kinds are way too interesting," Maud said.

"Oh?" Herb asked. "You thinking of anything in particular."

Maud sighed. "Never mind."

"Come on, Maud."

"You'd think when a woman gets to a certain age, men would lay back a little, enjoy life, not have to know everything."

"Here we go again, about men," Dennis said.

"What is it about men?" Ferguson asked.

Maud laughed, her voice husky and, if the truth be known, vibrant. She said, "Forget it, Fergie, not enough time for that. Huge topic."

Otis said, "New topic. I vote that Maud sing, at the dance."

Maud said, "Funny, you'd bring that up. I was deciding to do that."

"That's great, Maud," Sylvie said. "Why did you refuse to sing in Chadron? I asked you to, so did Dennis."

"Didn't feel like it. I don't know. Oh all right, I was scared."

"This time the vibes will be good," Dennis said. "I've got that feeling in my gut. I don't mean the Chadron gig wasn't okay, but this one, well, the thing is, we're ready now. We are really and truly ready." He looked at Howie. "Eh, piano man?"

Howie grinned. "I have that same feeling. Maud, what do you have in mind?"

"One by Tom Lehrer, from way back, but can't for the life of me remember all the words. Something about roaming the west, watching the sun go down, and there's a line about the FBI."

"I might be able to get it," Maureen said. "There's a guy here who's a sheet music and vinyl freak."

"You know this town?" Otis asled.

"I worked here quite a while, learned a few things about the food trade. Then there was an opening in Chadron. I bluffed my way in."

"I can believe that," Otis said.

The gym glowed in blue and green. Ferguson had done a masterful lighting job.

"Sea foam," Maud said. She was gowned in long green.

"Hey," Ferguson said, "you look like a husk of sweet corn."

"More like feed corn."

"Tough," he said, "but sweet."

They laughed together. Ferguson and the music makers mounted the stage. Dennis turned back, gave a helping hand to Maud. Ferguson went to the lighting board. The gym was filling fast. All ages, a good sign. Babs and Sylvie at the entrance handed out sea turtle singles.

Babs leaned to Sylvie. "Look at Maud, scared. I've never seen her like that."

Sylvie looked. "Babs, go up there, do something.."

"No, you go."

"Why me?"

"Because I'm no good at pep talk."

"Maybe that's not what she needs."

"Whatever it is, Maud needs it right now. You go. I'm serious. Go."

Sylvie went, up the side stairs and across the stage to the shadowed corner where Maud stood, her body unnaturally stiff, her face strained. "Sylvie, I can't do it."

"No, you'll do fine." That was pure blah blah, and Sylvie knew it.

"Tell George and Dennis I'm not up to it."

Sylvie put a timid hand on Maud's shoulder, felt the tension there, the bony hopelessness. She gripped harder, caught in a terrifying insight, that her own continuance was at stake, that she must fight for Maud, and for Breakout, or go under. "Maud, don't be this way."

"Easy for you to say."

A memory, like a blessing, came to Sylvie. "You remember something Otis said, back in Jonesport?"

"Otis said a lot of things."

"It was about us in the bus. We're old dogs, but we're re-inventing ourselves."

"I don't remember that."

Sylvie drew back. "Maud, I wouldn't lie to you. Besides, it's something I couldn't make up in a million years."

"Sylvie, I do appreciate what you're trying to do."

There was a slight condescension there. Sylvie couldn't overlook it. She turned stubborn, lifted her chin, looked directly into Maud's fierce eyes and another memory came. "You told me once, that we're old enough to damn near get past vanity. And I'm telling you now, you listen to me. Get off it. You hear me?"

Maud's hawklike face softened. "Oh god, I did say that, didn't I."

"You did. And don't forget, we're here for Breakout."

Sylvie felt Maud's body tremble, draw breath, become still. Another deep breath, and another.

"Go for it," Sylvie whispered.

George gave a hand signal to Ferguson, the doorway lights dimmed and Dennis stepped to the center mike. "Ladies and gentlemen, rascals and angels, are we ready?"

The crowd roared.

"I hope you have all, each one of you, paid admission. Each of you must have in your hand or in your pocket one sheet of essential sea turtle information. Let's hear it for those wandering reptiles, those grand ocean going travelers."

Cheers.

"I'll remind all you prairie people that admission to this grand celebration tonight is your promise to read about turtles. I don't want to see one single sheet in the trash barrel at the end of the festivities."

More cheers and then hands clapping. Howie hammered out the first bars of *Powder Milk Bisquits.*

Dennis shouted. *"Choose your partners,*

> *Clap for the grouse,*
> *Gird up your girdles*
> *Bring down the house."*

Dennis called two dances. George followed with a sentimental fiddle waltz to calm people down. As the last strains died Ferguson put a blue light at stage center and Maud stepped into it. Her voice quavered as she introduced her song. Otis, standing next to Maureen near the entrance, closed his eyes. Maureen was intensely aware of restiveness among the dancers. They were fiddle footed, impatient.

Otis had organized a claque: Maureen, Sylvie, Babs, Herb, Leonard, himself and the man who had found the Tom Lehrer lyrics on an old vinyl platter.

Maureen leaned to Otis, whispered, "I'm afraid."

"Don't be," he whispered, stifling his own doubts.

Maud stood silently tall and gaunt, looking into the crowd, sensing wavelets of disapproval. She began, a little too breathily and then courage came.

Along the trail you'll find me lopin'
Where the spaces are wide open,
In the land of the old A.E.C.
Where the scenery's attractive,
And the air is radioactive,
Oh, the Wild West is where I wanna be.

'Mid the sagebrush and the cactus
I'll watch the fellows practice

Droppin' bombs through the clean desert breeze.
   A-ha!
I'll have on my sombrero,
And of course I'll wear a pair of
Levis over my lead B.V.D.'s.

No squeaks. That was her abiding fear, that she'd drift too high and squeak. That's why she'd left out Lehrer's *Yee hoos*. She knew that the people out there were far from thrilled. She also knew, now, that she would finish the song, it would not be total disaster. She delivered the last verse in a frolicking growl.

Mid the yuccas and the thistles
I'll watch the guided missiles,
While the old FBI watches me.
Yes, I'll soon make my appearance
(Soon as I can get my clearance)
'Cause the Wild West is where I wanna be.

The claque burst into applause. Someone shouted "encore". Applause rippled through the dancers. Shouts of encore became insistent.

Dennis looked at George who shook his head. Ferguson mouthed "What the hell?" Dennis went to the piano, leaned down to whisper, "Howie, is this a conspiracy?"

"If there is I'm not in on it. People liked the song, that's all."

"So? What do we do?"

"Leave it to Maud. If she's got anything I'll plink-plunk along. You too. Quit worrying, Dennis, stuff like this happens all the time."

Maud stood steadfast in the blue circle. She managed to smile and that struck like a dart in Otis's chest. Maud was speaking.

"Thank you. I'd like to add a few verses I made up on the bus, traveling here. This is from Breakout, and *for* all the species, the living creatures out there…and here too. *That's* what Breakout is all about."

She began. Howie caught the drift right away. Dennis tapped on the guitar's body, George plucked gently on his G string. They stayed in low soft tones, where Maud's voice was best.

Here we are all hopin',
have a funny notion
when turtles keep on paddlin'
in the seas,
when whales keep on deep divin'
sharp-tails walk their prairies free
We might all be free.

The dancers started rhythmic clapping. Maud
dared to up her volume.

> *This funny notion*
> *a rather dark commotion*
> *tickling from my galoshes*
> *through the bones of all my losses*
> *to the crown of my gray hair.*
> *When turtles keep on paddlin'*
> *in the seas.*
> *When whales keep on deep divin'*
> *sharp-tails prairie walkin'*
> *We can all be free*
> *We can all be free.*

There was one little squeak in the last refrain,
but Maud didn't give a damn and neither did
anybody else.

Motel Downtown, Valentine

After the dance. Breakout travelers had
profited greatly from a day of rest and from
memories of the good job they'd done. Now they
were on duty again, going door-to-door with sea
turtle singles.

It was a beautiful morning. Maureen, turning onto the motel's parking space, saw an old woman on the shaded patio in rigid stillness, hands clenched in her lap. Maureen recognized her. Sylvie. A man was with her. Maureen knew him too; Leonard, driver of the Breakout bus.

Maureen called, "Good morning."

Sylvie didn't move, but Leonard looked up.

"Babs is gone," he said.

"Gone? Where? Oh."

Sylvie looked up, her eyes glistening. She drew a quavery breath. "Babs keeps forgetting her meds."

Leonard said "Babs went with Ferguson today, giving turtle sheets. Sylvie was tired, stayed here. Ferguson called my cell phone, from the hospital, talked crazy. I drove here, to tell Sylvie."

Maureen said, "I'll find a pharmacy, for a sedative." Leonard told her he had some. He ran to the bus, returned with a small plastic box and a bottle of spring water. He knelt and gave Sylvie water and a pill.

Maureen asked, "Where are the others?"

"Giving turtle sheets."

"Hell with that, round them up, they should all be here…oh, excuse me Leonard, I didn't mean to be so …"

"It's all right," he said.

As Leonard drove the bus onto the main street the realization hit hard. He had lost a friend. Babs, Sylvie, Leonard, a trio on the bus, whiling away many a road mile, talking of this and that, reminiscing, teasing. Babs the outspoken one, hilarious, outrageous. She stirred the banter, brought Leonard and Sylvie out of their accustomed caution. Babs and Sylvie, a great pair. Leonard had come to suspect that neither of them believed in God. He wasn't offended by that, though he wondered how anyone could survive without faith. Would Sylvie survive?

Motel Downtown's patio was crowded. Breakout travelers tight-lipped, not knowing how to act, what to say. Maureen felt out of place. She slipped away and walked the main street of Valentine, a town she knew well, but today it seemed strange, distant. She came to Valentine's doggy diner and stopped there to look into the fringes of town. What would the world be like without sharp-tailed grouse? One smidgeon better? Or worse? Who gives a rat's ass? What is this world, anyway? What matters? She went into the diner.

Bert Gill, freelance carpenter, sat at the counter. She took the stool on his left. He was about to dig into a heavy platter of ham and home fries, but noticed Maureen. "Well, well, look who's here. Been a long time. I hear things about you."

"Probably all true," she said. "Bert, talk to me."

"Something happen?"

"One of the Breakout people is dead."

"One of the old ones?"

"Yes, one of them."

"They put on one hell of a dance."

"Yes." She put her head on the counter and quivered and shed tears and Bert put his hand on her shoulder and did his best with words.

Near dark. Intermittent whiffs of warm wind.

They gathered beyond the edge of town to say a few words, but no one knew how to begin. Were they thinking that no words were needed, that their collective silence was the best way to honor Babs? No, they were humans, after all. Words were required.

Sylvie spoke. "I met Babs at Maple View. She saved me, she really did." Sylvie consideried telling about Babs' early life, the terrible things, but no, those were secrets, those were tokens of friendship, nobody else's business. She yearned to find a way to explain how her friend had made a life out of shambles, a valiant comeback, and how that had become a gift, for others. No, she couldn't. Instead, she talked about Babs knowing practically nothing about species, but she knew people. And she was forgetful. Sometimes her mind went someplace else, but when she came back she'd look around and you could see she was bright as a new penny."

Silence again, woven into the casual wind.

Leonard said, "Babs, you made fun of all of us. Nobody got away."

Otis lifted his head, noticed Leonard standing about a stride and a half away from everyone else. Otis remembered Leonard and Babs and Sylvie in earnest or playful interchanges at the front of the bus. Otis felt the touch of the wind and the scent of disturbed prairie land and he told himself that there was still life to be lived, to be undergone. "Babs," he said, "we're here to honor you, not to say goodbye. There's more work to be done and we're tired, but we'll do it and you will be with us." It sounded a mite pompous, Otis thought. Almost doctrinal, but so be it, and whatever gods there be, take notice that we are worn to the bone. He said, "Let's go back to Grayling."

Breakout bus, third day on the road. approaching Grayling. Ferguson, across the aisle from Maud, had been thinking about her and the encore she had sung, about freedom. Of course freedom was an American thing, but hooked into sea turtles and whales? Ferguson was trying to wrap his mind around that, trying for a clue that might lead to the secret heart of Breakout, its core, its danger.

He crossed to the empty seat next to Maud. "Great show back there, Maud. You were great."

"I did what I could," she said. "I give myself a B minus."

"No, honestly, you were great."

"You don't have to say that."

Ferguson began to sputter that he meant every word of it, but Maud laid a hand on his shoulder and gripped hard. "Thanks, but we both know better. I feel good about it and we pulled it off okay. The dancers had fun, took the turtle sheets, went away happy. You be glad to get home?"

"Well, yes and no. This traveling and putting on shows, it's all brand new to me. Getting back into harness in Grayling, I don't know, sort of a letdown, I guess."

"I saw you with that hair-down-to-her-waist blonde, in Valentine."

"Yeah, well, she dragged me off the stage. I was clumsy, but I don't think that bothered her too much."

"She was having fun, I could tell."

"So was I, actually. I sort of got the hang of it. Maud, there's something I've been wanting to ask you. Otis wondered if I'd be organizer for a gig in Grayling, since I know the town. What do you think?"

"You'd be good at it, Fergie, but right now give us a couple days rest. Otis especially, he's taken on too much."

"You notice things, Maud, about people."

"I'll tell you something, Fergie. In a nursing home you get to know people. Too well, actually. There''s all the ailments and sadness and break-downs, and then, it's funny…I don't mean hah, hah funny…at the same time there's hardly anything going on. You get so you notice little things."

"Like what, Maud? Give me an example., secrets behind the secrets."

She looked around. Otis and Herb asleep, Sylvie looking out the window, Leonard's strong shoulders squared against the night: headlights, tail lights, brake lights. He must be tired too. "Never mind," she said, "you'll find out, thirty, forty years down the road." But she relented, having a sudden vision of herself at nineteen, svelte and lively and in on everything. "Fergie, you won't believe this, I was once a model."

"Oh, I can believe that."

"For about a week, then it was over. Too much bosom and not enough zip to my nose."

Ferguson thought about his wife's long, thin nose, and her mouth that he still thought of as the perfect rosebud, and her eyes, deep and dark. "Zip?"

"Look around, Fergie. Things haven't changed that much. The secret behind the secret, if you really want to know, is not all that secret. A person doesn't get into these big public places like TV and films and all that if you have too much of this or not enough of that, or if you're too old, or too, I don't know…too anything. My nose was…*pronounced* was the word they used. High, wide and handsome, that was me, in those days."

To: BREAKOUT@LISTSERV.SPEAKOUT.ORG
From: lgrady@westelcom.com
Re: Water

I work for U.S. Forest Service, have some acquaintnce with animals and vegetation and water anf fire. Here are some pieces of bad news from The Land Institute based in Salina, Kansas:

"... the Arkansas and Smoky Hill rivers no longer flow in Western Kansas. Sewage effluent from Great Bend, Kansas often serves as the headwaters of the Arkansas river. Drilled wells for irrigation pump at 1,000 gallons per minute from the aquifer."

We and the animals, such as grouse and prairie dogs and range cattle and all the others are in this together. This linkage is not an opinion. This linkage is a fact.

In parts of eastern Colorado and western Kansas and Nebraska more than a 50 to 100 foot drop has occured in the aquifer level. Kansas Geological Survey estimates that pumping rates would have to decrease by more than 80 percent before sustainable levels of pumping can be reached."

Arizona's water problems are even worse.

Harvey Boshardt met them on the parking lot. Effusive welcomes were not his way, but he hustled around, telling them to not worry about luggage, he'd bring it all in as soon as Leonard had the bay open. He offered a nightcap. Coffee, or something stronger? They didn't seem to know what they wanted.

Leonard opened the bay, began hauling out baggage. He told Harvey that sleep would probably be the best for everyone. Harvey noticed Sylvie standing alone, looking terribly sad. He went to her. "I don't see your partner."

"She died." Sylvie stared at the gravelled ground, found herself leaning against Harvey and catching her breath in little sniffles that turned into a long howl.

Harvey held her for a few moments, then escorted her to No. 3. unlocked it with his master key. waited for her to limp inside. He turned on the bedside lamp. Maud stood in the doorway. "I'll stay with her tonight."

"All right."

Leonard noticed Ferguson slipping away without a word, and Howie lugging his duffle bag into his pickup. Leonard knew that Howie had a gig a few days hence, but he'd be in touch. Leonard noticed also that the stars were out in unusual splendor, that the night was still and mild.

Maud followed Otis to the door of his motel unit. "You all right?"

Fumbling, he unlocked the door. "Tired, a little confused. Do you ever lose track of everything you just said a minute ago?"

"My mind cuts out on me all the time. Old model, cranky, unreliable, needs work."

"I'm thinking maybe I'm not up to this activist life any more."

"You're doing fine, get some rest. Good night."

"Goodnight, Maud, you're a peach."

George and Dennis and Leonard had been given a collective name, "The Youngsters," by Babs, in recognition of their being "under sixty." The tag stuck and now the three so honored sometimes used it themselves. They were always the first to show up at Rita's Place, two and a half blocks from Quiet Pines, for breakfast, followed closely by Otis. They made a regular quartet and were being gradually assimilated into the talkative crowd of workers on the way to work. All was as usual, on this bright blue morning, except that Otis didn't show up. When Maud came in for her coffee and toast George asked, "Is Otis out birding?"

"Not that I know of," Maud said, then stood still, struck by a premonition. She shook it off, but it came back. Last night Otis had looked utterly worn out; that was nothing new, but his loss of confidence was something she'd never seen before. "George, cancel my order, I forgot something."

She returned to Quiet Pines and knocked on Otis's door and listened. Nothing. She tried the doorknob, the door swung open. Maud took two steps and knew, again, death.

Otis lay on the bed fully dressed except for shoes and socks, his face turned to the ceiling. Maud touched his forehead and wrist. She went outside and called for help.

Xenia, Ohio.

Rufus stood in the crowded spaces between tables in Linda's Restaurant, looking for Lawrence Buell. He was interrupted by a low buzzing from his jacket pocket. Puzzled, he reached in, touched the cell phone Enid had given him. Peering closely, he located a button that appeared to be the one to punch to receive. It was Enid. Had he heard abut Otis?

"No, what happened?"

She told him, tearfully, but Rufus stayed dry-eyed and still, watching a bare wall, watching a part of his life steal away in the mingle of food odors and early morning breakfast racket. He said, "Thank you, Enid," and hung up.

Waiters edged past him. The bustle and noise gave some comfort. He remembered his appointment, here at Linda's. He considered canceling, but recoiled from the prospect of being alone. He went to the nearest booth and asked the four men there if they knew a Lawrence Buell. One of them did. "You're in luck, over there, youngish guy with the neat pointy beard."

Yesterday, in a long distance call from Akron, Rufus had found Buell in his office. The conversation had been short and not sweet.

"I'm from Breakout. You posted a brief note on our list."

"You'll find me around noon at Linda's Restaurant, Xenia. About ten or twenty steps from Detroit and Main. Can't have you meeting me at work, don't want you at home either. If you insist on a meeting, come to Linda's."

Rufus looked around, spotted his man, managed to catch his eye. He drew both hands to his chest. Buell waited till a story wound down. Hearty guffaws. Rufus heard Buell say, "See you guys later, got to see this man about a dog." He rose, took a few steps, posed in front of Rufus, hands in pockets.

"You called me about Breakout."

"Yes. I'm Rufus Knutson."

Buell said, "Somebody at your end fucked up. I was not in distress, did not ask for Breakout to send someone to check up on me."

"Okay," Rufus said. He didn't care, he was numb. Ashes to ashes.

"As a matter of fact" Buell said, "I rather enjoyed my chat with the federals."

"Okay."

"My backchannel message to you people was a warning to the innocents who might be entangled in whatever you people are up to." He raised his voice, other voices quit or dwindled. "You might be an innocent. From your age I'd guess you are. No doubt you fail to realize what you're mixed up in. I have to tell you, Breakout has a dubious backgkround. As such, it poses a danger."

"You're a lawyer," Rufus said.

"And a damned good one."

"I'm sure, and I'll lay you a twenty to your one, the feds sweet talked you, suggested you work with them for the greater glory of national security and the Patriot Act."

The restaurant's buzz and clamor had quieted so much by now that Rufus's retort, though given in his normal voice, could be heard as far back as the kitchen's swinging door.

Buell sputtered. "Don't use that tone with me. I'll repeat, and you pay attention. My messsage to Breakout was meant as a warning, letting you know you're under surveillance, a matter of courtesy. That's it, end of story."

"No," Rufus said, "that's the beginning of story. The feds will be back for another nice little talk with you. In the meantime, what you sent Breakout was a little package of worry. Nice going, the feds will appreciate that. Spreading worry, they like that."

Buell roared. "Listen you old geezer, you're crossing the line here, this interview is over. Get the fuck out of my face."

"And fuck you too," Rufus said, "and the horse you rode in on." He whirled, staggered, recovered, grabbed for the heavy glass door, heaved it open, walked out. "Otis, what would you have done? You'd have given him hell too. But with style. That's what you had, old man, a way all your own." He crossed the busy street, ignoring traffic, made it to the courthouse lawn and leaned against a tree.

To: BREAKOUT@LISTSERV.SPEAKUP.ORG

From: calbock@frontienet.net

Re: Flower loving fly

Heard a lawyer for developers complain on NPR today, that half of California's privately owned land is classified by Fish and Wildlife as "critical habitat." Something wrong with that? I'm surprised the feds had the guts to come right out and say that all the thousands of other species might have some slight claim to as much as half of what this one species, H. sapiens, thinks it owns.

I agree with Echo, something REALLY different has to happen.

Cal

Leaving Xenia, Rufus decided to bypass Betsy Truro, the third and last of the people whose names Enid had given him, but when he came to Ohio 72 he turned right instead of left and soon found himself parking at the campus of Cedarville University. Going from one group of students to another, asking for Betsy, he soon realized he was on the pleasant and quiet grounds of a Christian institution. Might it be a good idea to stop prowling around, take time out to stop, be quiet, come to terms with Otis's death? Or pray? Why not, Rufus? You prayed when Hilde was near death, didn't you? He honestly couldn't remember whether his bitter mumblings then had held something of prayer in them.

He wandered on. Students treated him politely. Some of them knew Betsy, but not her present whereabouts. He did find her, seated on the ground under a white oak, in earnest conversation with a youth her age. Her hair was coal black, her eyes a light hazel. When Rufus introduced himself she rose and brushed at her skirt. "Oh, thiis is Lyle."

Lyle said, "Glad to meet you, sir."

Betsy led the way to two nearby benches that were angled toward each other in the scanty shade of a black locust, a beautiful tree hung with ripening seed pods and crisp late summer leaves on dark branches.

"I am so glad you came," Betsy said. "I was confused. I still am, can't even remember if they told me if they were FBI or some other branch of homeland security."

"Don't blame yourself," Lyle said. "

"I'm not blaming myself, I am stating the condition of my mind."

"I keep urging you, Betsy," Lyle said, "to go deeper, you'll find a place of safety."

"Oh I don't know," Rufus said. "Hard to tell what's safe these days. Deep sounds good, but sometimes it's pretty shallow."

"I'm speaking of a spiritual place," Lyle said.

"I know you are." He turned to Betsy. "You're a senior?"

"How did you know?"

"Just a guess. The way you talk, holding two ideas in mind at once."

"Really? Anyway, whoever they were, those federal people, I can't fault them. A man and a woman, very respectful, but I couldn't understand why they were talking to me, of all people. I mean, Lyle and I, he's a senior too, got on the Breakout listserv because we've been studying rattlesnakes, down in Spring Valley, catching them and marking them, helping out in a project at Wright State."

"We want to back up the claim that this subspecies of *Sistrurus* is endangered," Lyle said.

Rufus said. "Rattlesnakes, that's interesting. Betsy, can you remember your visitors making any specific statements, or requests?"

"They used one word a lot: *help*. Like, 'You can be a great help.' They asked if they might contact me later. I said they could. Wish now I hadn't."

Lyle said. "I think they thought just because we are Christians we would think environmentalists are next door to terrorists."

"I can imagine them believing that," Rufus said.

"They'd be wrong," Lyle said. "We have faith, we believe in Jesus and we're environmentnalists, Betsy and I."

"Because of the rattlesnakes," Betsy said. "We caught them with forked sticks and then held them to make measurements and mark them."

"Dangerous," Rufus said.

She smiled. "We were careful. When I first took hold of one I felt its scales and how strong it was; it wiggled and twisted and the strangest feeling came over me, like how it was, wanting to live. Oh, I can't explain it."

"Jesus spoke of *the least of these*," Lyle said.

Rufus said, "Goddammit, excuse my French, Lyle, but I've got to inform you, rattlesnakes are not the least of anything. They're themselves. They're set up to struggle in this miserable world, like all the rest of us, but rattllesnakes are different and so are we."

Lyle stayed cool. "It's not a miserable world, it's God's own."

Rufus looked up into the locust branches. Beautiful against the sky, but no comfort there. Day of misery. He looked at Lyle and shook his head. He pushed himself from the bench. "Betsy, I don't know what to tell you. The main thing is to not let anybody do your thinking for you."

Betsy asked, "Where's your car?"

He pointed to the far edge of the campus.

She said, "I'll walk with you. Lyle, I'll catch you at the caf." She walked away with quick steps. Rufus gave Lyle a little wiggle of a wave and limped after Betsy. She waited for him, in the shade of another locust.

She said, "You don't like Lyle."

"What makes you think that?"

"It sticks out all over. Come on, Rufus, be honest."

"Well," he said, "none of this is any of my business."

"You've made it your business, by your coming here, and by your attitude, but I'm glad for straight talk. Here's some more that isn't your business: My dad died last year, my mom is holding down a minimum wage job, my brother is in the navy, and war hangs over us."

They walked on. She said, "And you think I'm too dependent on Lyle."

"Do I?"

"It's plain as anything."

"I do depend on Lyle. I'm confused so much of the time."

"Lyle could use some of that."

"Some of what?"

"Confusion."

"That's a strange thing to say."

They walked on.

"Seems perfectly natural to me,"Rufus said. "Confusion. The world is built that way. I bet your rattlesnakes would agree. I remember watching a garter snake working up a chain of little rapids and waterfalls. Trying to reach high ground, I suppose, but of course I didn't know what it really had in mind. Why not go down hill? Quite a sight, seeing that snake try a certain way and get thrown back by the flow of water or by losing its grip, and then it would try another way and sometimes get a chinhold, just like you or me wold get a handhold. Then it would hitch itself up, make a little progress and then check out the next problem."

"Did it get there?"

"It did, until I lost sight of it. Had no idea, of course, what getting there meant to a snake."

"Is this some kind of parable you're handing me?"

"Oh good lord no. Not exactly sure what a parable is. Just talking about snakes. About confusion, maybe."

They came to his car. He took the keys from his pocket and she said, "Thank you for taking the trouble.. Thank you very much," and she touched his arm and then she was against him and he held her, feeling comforted.

Rufus found I-70 and turned toward Indianapolis and points west. He knew what he was doing, though barely admitting it. Two days of driving brought him to Chadron, Nebraska. Early evening. He parked and stood on the curb wondering how he might manage to happen to run into Maureen. He walked to the corner, looked down the cross street and there it was. Joseph's Restaurant. The lettering was plain. No neon. He went in and was escorted to a two-person table under a paneled wall that displayed a large print of a ten-horse team pulling a wheat harvester. Rufus admired it. Colors of ripened wheat, multi-colored horses, a dynamic yet soothing scene. He tried to make out the signature. When a waiter brought his coffee he asked if Maureen worked there. The waiter studied him for a coiuple of blinks. "She's the manager."

"Yes. I'm Just passing through, wanted to say hello, that's all."

"I'll see if she's in."

He looked at the painting again and then Maureen was there. "Well, well, the wanderer returns."

He stood up, clumsily. The hard driving had stiffened him badly. They shook hands. She said, "You could have given me a call."

"Yup, could have."

She laughed. "Do you mind if I have dinner with you? Remember Bordeaux Trading Post? I promised you a treat. The special tonight is broiled swordfish."

"Wow. That's kind of crazy."

"Endangered species? Politically incorrect? Just this once, please. And wine? Let me order, I'd like you to try a good dry wine, an Ontario vintage. Ice wine."

"Didn't know Ontario had a vintage."

"They do, near the lakes, mild climate."

For a few fleeting moments they contemplated each other. Then Maureen rushed on, with news of the Sharp-tail Festival. "We did pretty well, I danced with Otis."

"Otis? Danced?"

"I persuaded him. He was a good sport about that, and then the music took over."

"The music took over. Good lord." Rufus looked away. "Otis died," he said.

"No."

"In his sleep. Good way to go."

"We talked, just a little, after the dance. He mentioned you. More than a mention, said you were sound, you had sand, but stubborn as a Scandihoovian ox."

"Huh. Otis was stubborn as they come."

"You were friends, I could tell."

He looked up at the ten-horse team. Maureen signalled a waiter. She ordered.

Rufus asked, "Who's the artist?"

"Art Coelho, in Montana. It's a print. I bought it myself. We needed color in here. All this dark paneling."

They swirled and sniffed and tasted the wine and Rufus said it was better than Gallo. They toasted the Breakout travelers. Rufus muttered, "Bunch of tottery old ducks, dropping off, one by one."

"I am so sad, about Otis."

Rufus nodded, but thought about war. Bad habit. So often, in moments of near bliss, as now with Maureen in the subdued humm of conversation in a town, Chadron, that he'd come to like, war moved in on him. A century of war, was the way he looked at the twentieth. And for what? And another century opening with the same stupid horrors, revved up now, to the nth power.

The attack faded. He saw that Maureen was looking at him, questioning, and he wondered where she was in the march of time with hair so beautifully fluffed, a wavy darkness streaked with silver, and two silver bracelets on her left wrist and a turqoise set in silver on her right hand little finger. Mid sixties? What was it like, way back there? He tried to recall, to feel, the physicality of what it had been like.

She said, "I turned sixty six last week. I'm thinking of retiring."

"Good idea."

They spoke of families. Maureen's only daughter lived in Santa Fe, married to a gallery owner who specialized in gaudy paintings of big-hatted cowboys, Indian warriers and huge animals equipped with remendous claws or teet or horns. "He doesn't understand her," was Maureen's complaint.

Rufus's two offspring were far away, one in California, the other in Washington state. He confessed to a recurring question: Where was he when they were young and at home? Why did he feel he had done nothing for them other than make the mortgage payments and buy things?"

"Those are normal ways of looking back." Maureen said.

He remembered her unfinished novel, her giving up on the possibility of recapturing life in those years. March of time, leaving nothing but confusion. War after war.

Again, she was studying him, and he knew it.

And the time came for parting. It was difficult. They said they'd keep in touch. Maureen gave him a hug. He turned it into a tight embrace. Then he was gone, limping toward quiet night time traffic.

At the car Rufus fitted key to lock, noticed a slight bulge in his jacket pocket. Cell phone, reminding him of his one fumbly use of it, to call Quiet Pines and talk to Harvey Boshardt about last rites for Otis. Boshardt had made most of the arrangements. Rufus had begged off attending, claiming an urgent meeting in Nebraska. Boshardt accepted that without a murmur. "Simple memorial service, in the woods. People say a few words, if they've a mind to. No preaching. Scatter ashes. That's the way my tenants want it. I could put some wild flowers there, Rufus, in your name. Got some real nice tall asters out back."

"Harvey, I'd be eternally grateful to you." He meant it.

Rufus's next remembrance was that he owed Enid a call. He looked at his watch; eight thirty here in Chadron, Mountain Daylight Time, same in Wyoming. He consulted his notebook, found Enid's phone number and punched it in. She answered.

"Hi, Enid, I'm in Chadron, Nebraska. I got in touch with those three names you gave me."

"Oh good, how did they go?"

"A mixed bag. Interesting." He gave her an abbreviated account of his meetings with Charlie Anderson in Vermont, Lawrence Buell and Becky Truro in Ohio.

Enid said, "It was a good thing to do, don't you think?"

"Oh sure, I'm glad you pushed for it."

"You must be exhausted."

"I'm fine."

"Rufus, there's something I need to tell you, a decision I made. On a certain Saturday soon I will go to where the highway to Sabille canyon meets U.S. 30 and stand there with a sign that will read STOP WAR, or words to that effect."

"Good."

"Is that all you have to say?"

"I could say a lot, don't get me started."

"Yes, I know, Rufus dear, but what would you yourself think if a woman in Lemmon, South Dakoa called you and said to you that she and two other women up there are going to stop war and they want your help?"

"What kind of help?"

"The kind I just described, standing with a sign, on a highway."

"Hmmm."

"I see. Your reaction would be that maybe you would, but it would be just another effort worthy of praise, but nothing more than a gesture."

"Enid, what's this all about?"

She told him.

"A *showing*," he said. It started playing to him; it set off a little flare, a ringing.

"You there, Rufus?"

"Lemmon, you say?"

"Yes, near the Grand river, next to North Dakota border."

"I think I better get up there and talk to those folks."

"Oh, would you? That would be marvelous."

He sat there looking through the windshield, Chadron traffic a meaninglesss blur. He said, "I'll call you from Lemmon." He switched off and got out of the car, left it unlocked, hurried back to Joseph's, breathing hard. He barged in, interrupted the hostess who was escorting a foursome to a table. "Maureen, is she still here?"

The hostess recognized him, the manager's companion, but that didn't mean he was entitled to special favors. She pointed, decisively. "Sir, please go back there and wait."

Rufus obeyed. He stood in quivering impatience, talking sense to himself, to no avail.

The hostess returned. "She might have gone home, I'm not sure."

"I have to contact her, it's important."

"Sure, but it's not the end of the world."

Maureen appeared, standing well aside from the to-and-fro kitchen traffic. Rufus waved. Maureen threaded her way through the turmoil of prime time dining.

"I have to talk to you," Rufus said.

She led him to a clear space, behind the cashier's desk.

"Something's come up,," he said.

"Breakout?"

"Yes, sort of." He told her about the Lemmon project. The cashier listened in. Rufus admitted that he'd made a rash promise, to go to Lemmon.

Maureen was growing more and more impatient. "Why are you telling me all this?"

"It's important."

"I agree. Wouldn't mind standing with a sign myself." She was watching him like a cat at a vole's runway. Confusion swept over him. No, it was failure of courage. He managed to ask if she had ever been to Lemmon, South Dakota.

"Never heard of it."

"Me neither," the cashier said.

Maureen cast her a half humorous look, zeroed in on Rufus again. "Goddammit, Rufus, are you asking me to go with you or are you not?"

"Oh my," the cashier murmured.

"I'm asking," he said.

"Now?"

He hesitated and she said, "Tonight?"

Again he hesitated. "Soon."

She said, "Give me an hour."

He smiled till it hurt.

Lemmon, South Dakota.

To: SDROUNDTABLE@LISTSERV.TALK.ORG

  (and 57 others)

From: lemwarstop@earthlink.com

Re: Stop War

The time has come to put all our cards on the table. You are sick of war and sick of getting ready for war and how it never ever ends. And you know it doesn't solve a damn thing. It makes everything worse for all of us and we mean ALL OF US living creatures of the earth, all. If you do not know how terrible the destructions on this good earth have been brought about by war, then you are ignorant and you had better start educating yourself.

And another thing, if you do know about these destructions and sit on your butt and don't rise up to stop them, then you are fooling yourself. Yes, you are. We are telling you to your face that you are pulling a fast one on yourself. Take that and put it in your pipe and smoke it.

In this 21st century we know, even if we almost always don't say it, that killing from a distance is scattershot tragedy. People free and brave treat each other better than that.

Here is what can be done. On a certain Saturday, very soon, each one of us takes a nice big sign that you have made yourself and you take that sign to a place where one highway meets another and you stand there from seven in the morning till nine. Take a break. Go home or go somewhere to talk things over with whoever is with you. Talk about what happened, think carefully about every little thing, then go back for noon hour traffic. That's all you have to do.

These standings will be happening all across our nation. We are the ones who make this nation. We are the ones. We will be showing each other where we stand. Words are not enough and you know this as well as we do. No excuses. Just put your body out there. This will be a grand showing, FOR US.

Not for TV, not for the rulers, not for experts who are not out there with us, not for anybody who thinks they can boost their selfish egos by making fun of us.

You are thinking this showing will not stop war. You are right, it won't. We will set another date, another weekend date so you can't say sorry, have to work, sorry, have to go to class. We will stand again, each little group of us will learn how to do it better in the next show. And the next and the next. We will find ways to do it. We will learn. We will not do it perfectly the first time.

Are you ready? Somebody has to set the date. We will let you know.

WARNING: Do not waste time hoping a TV truck will visit you, or hoping that CNN will give us a decent showing. Hoping like that is a downer. This is OUR show. We will be telling each other about how it went and how we can do better. Don't get down on your knees. Stand proud on your own two feet. If you are disabled, get out there anyway; bully somebody to get you there. Show up!!!

To: BREAKOUT@LISTSERV.SPEAKUP.ORG

From: blandfair@erinet.com

Re: Dance

Dear one and all at Breakout. I was at the contra dance put on here in Valenine. It was wonderful, and different! The caller, the woman who sang about freedom, the lively music, everything. Thank you so much.

bev

Leonard moved the bus into the motel's back yard, putting it in shade and warm smell of pine. They met there, another strategy session, what to do about the challenge from South Dakota.

Herb was still questioning himself about what he had said at Otis's memorial meeting, scarcely believing his own words that had praised Otis's dedication to doing the right thing, no matter what. Herb had held in his mind an inconvenient truth, that he had disliked Otis, and yet another truth, their forced companionship, the Maple View Crocks on their own in the wide world, forced to work out solutions, minds and bodies in action. All of that in spite of failing physiologies, pampered by little caches of pharmaceuticals that sometimes did help. Herb stood now in Otis's place, on the second-from-the-top step, wondering if he ought to be there. "This message from Lemmon, South Dakota," he said. "What's our pleasure?"

Immediaely, Maud spoke, her growl resonant in the bus's confines. "We all know war is out of date, it's just plain silly, blowing up things, killing people for no good reason, no good reason at all. Let's find a place where crazy traffic has to slow down and look people right square in the face with our own wornout faces. This is the chance of a lifetime."

Dennis mumbled to George. "Maybe it's time we cleared out."

"Can't just up and do that."

"Why not? We didn't sign on for the duration. Besides, your family and mine have been asking a lot of questions. Who do we think we are, traveling around the country in a bus, far from home, hawking sea turtles in Michigan and Nebraska?"

They'd gone over these matters, lying in the dark at Quiet Pines, talking to the ceiling. But the Lemmon thing had caught them by surprise. From endangered species to anti-war, quite a jump, hard to fathom.

Herb called to them. "Can't hear you guys."

"Oh, we were just wondering if maybe we ought to go back to tide waters, where we belong," Dennis said.

But George softened that. "We haven't decided yet. Might be fun to paint a great big whale on the side of this bus and a bunch of seagoing turtles on the other side and maybe a grouse on the rear and go out there and join the showing."

Sylvie spoke, about whales hunted by the *Pequod* and the other whaling ships, for oil. It had been all about oil. Thoughtless of the future, men had set out to harvest the bounty of the seas. "It's still about oil,," she said.

"Yes, but what's your position, Sylvie?" Herb asked. "Yes or no, on the Lemmon thing?"

"Yes," she said.

Maud boomed. "There's two of us, for a great big YES. And I say yes for big animals painted on the bus."

"Three of us," George said, and Dennis looked at him in alarm, and then shrugged and studied his hands.

Ferguson was thrilled. Here at long last the secret agenda behind the species shield: anti-war. But something else gave him pause; every person on the bus was thinking hard about "Yes" or "No." Ferguson had come to know these Breakout travelers; he knew that each one, by way of individual struggle, was reaching toward a decision. They weren't exactly acting like innocents manipulated from afar. "I'm of two minds about this," he said. "Can we trust those Lemmon women?"

Herb, his arguments with Otis coming to the fore, couldn't resist a half serious remark. "How about Breakout? Can we trust those women? What's really going on back there in Rock River?"

Dennis said, "Doesn't matter whether we trust Enid and Jennifer and Rufus, or those Lemmon people. Point is, somebody's come up with an interesting thing to do. I'm almost inclined to go along with George, after all. Let's give it a try. But dammit, George, what's my wife going to say?"

"My wife already knows I'm not reliable," George said.

Silence, Herb looking around. "What's your take on this, Leonard?"

"Si, se puede," Leonard said.

"Which means?"

Leonard smiled, but there was a slight lift of his shoulders, signifying that nothing is certain in this world. "It means, 'Yes, we can do it.'"

Quiet Pines.

Sylvie, basking in morning sunlight. She had painfully dragged a chair from her motel unit and poked its spindly legs securely into parking lot gravel.Closing her eyes against the sun, she relapsed into the vibrant fantasyland that made up a good part of her life. A familiar voice kept intruding. She ignored it until the voice said, clearly, "Jennifer …"

Sylvie opened her eyes, located the voice inside the motel office. Fergie's.

"...Jennifer, haven't yet met her. Maybe she's the one. They're going all out for this Lemmon Alliance stop war business now, did you know that?"

Another voice, Harvey Boshardt's. "Al, give it up. I'm telling you, these old folks are harmless. They spend their last days going around the country handing out these sheets of paper; nothing wrong with that, might even do some good. I have a kind of admiration for what they're doing."

"Yes, Harvey, I feel the same way, but *what's behind it all*, that's what I'm taking all this trouble to find out."

"Al, you're chasing your own tail with all this behind the behind stuff."

"I'm a patriot, that's why."

"Quit saying that to me. You think I'm not a patriot?"

"I think no such thing."

'Then shut up about it. You've got to use your own judgement on this thing."

"That's exactly what I'm doing."

"I don't think so. The guy you're reporting to, and don't go thinking I don't know who it is by now, you're the one doing all this underground sleuthing around and he sits there like a big old barn spider in a web, expecting you patriots to bring him some shady stuff for him to pass on to whatever bigger barn spider he's beholden to."

"That's quite a speech, Harvey. Don't think I've ever heard you sound off like that."

"Go ahead, report it."

"Aw come on, for Christ sake."

Sylvie, leaning precariously toward the office door, waited for more. She heard a loud sigh from Fergie, and then, "The damndest thing is, Harvey, I don't know when I've been getting such a kick out of life."

Sylvie waited until she was alone with Maud before speaking about what she'd heard. Maud, smug as a bug, said, "I always thought there was something a little off-kilter about Fergie. You might have noticed, he doesn't know a damn thing about sturgeons. They're his animal of special concern. He thinks they're all one species."

"That's not so terrible, Maud. I don't think Herb knows anything about whitebark pine, either, and Babs never ever posted on the Break-out list."

"I don't post on it either," Maud said, "but I used to read it, back in Maple View.

"Fergie's a spy. Isn't that amazing? We've got ourselves a spy."

"Let's keep quiet about it, for now."

"But he was really pissed at not having anything bad to report. What if he gets so frustrated he makes something up?"

"He might just do that, but if we expose him he's even more likely to turn sour. Actually, I sort of enjoy having him around."

To: BREAKOUT@LISTSERV.SPEAKUP.ORG

From: h2h@westelcom.com

Re: Lemmon

I work with Riverkeeper on the Hudson river, pressuring governments and corporations to clean up this great river. And education work too, especially with young people.

I don't want to jeopardize my work by having anything to do with this far left Lemmon affair.

Hal

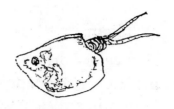

Springfield, Illinois.

Local Lemmon organizers rented a near-derelict ballroom, Prairie Rose, a remnant from the big band era. Two of the organizers happened to be lurkers on the Breakout list. They volunteered to scare up a few musicians. An invitation went to the Breakout travelers in Grayling. It was promptly accepted.

To: BREAKOUT@LISTSERV.SPEAKUP.ORG

From: mweis@mountainlink.com

Re: Lemmon

Hal, you're saying your Riverkeeper work would be jeopardized if you became known as a peacenik? Last I heard, Pete Seeger, that old extreme left banjo player, is a leading Riverkeeper. What the hay?

As for me, I thought up a bushel of excuses for myself. None of them held water. I'm going to make a sign and find me a highway junction. Peace, Mort

Grayling, Michigan.

Harbor View travelers arrived the day after those from Maple View had made their decision to support the Lemmon anti-war alliance. It was a nervous gathering, held in the brand new meeting place Harvey Boshardt had fixed up, in his garage behind Quiet Pines.

No one mentioned Lemmon, a topic best left for later.

Sam, as was his habit, made no attempt to hide his disdain for anything he judged tainted by complacency. Herb, picking up on those strong activist vibes, tagged him as an Otis type, but much more volatile. Maud and Sylvie kept a close eye on Helen, who was in a hyper state, edging toward hysteria. Sam's and Helen's partner, Paul Gallegos, waited for an explosion. Sam or Helen, one or the other, would trigger it. Paul braced himself.

The Youngsters, George, Dennis and Leonard, having busied themselves with luggage and assignments to motel units, appeared alert and calm.

George showed Helen and Sam the sea turtle singles, explained how they'd gone about delivering them, in Maine and now in Grayling. "Face to face, one on one. Conversation. Discussion."

Sam liked the tactic, but said it wasn't enough. "We have to go all out, use every lever."

Dennis wanted to know what would be enough.

Sam said, "Find ways to be ever more bold."

Helen exploded. "Christ all mighty, Sam, *bold* is a word, that's all it is. All this talk, talk, talk. I'm sick of it."

Sam shook his head, sadly and was about to speak when Harvey Boshardt came in noisily, kneeing open the door and sidling through with a tray that held lemonade, glasses, and chocolate chip cookies. He put the tray on the table. "There's more where that came from."

"Thanks a whole bunch, Harvey," Maud said.

Paul thanked him too.

Sam asked, "Do you have any ideas of your own, about extinction of species?"

Helen visisbly shuddered. Paul didn't like it either.

"I'm glad the wolves are back," Harvey said.

"Why?" Sam asked.

Harvey had his own survival reasons for being kind and generous to this particular flock. Stable occupancy every night to the end of the year and with an option to renew. Reason enough, but there was more. Harvey had observed them, overheard conversations and arguments. He had taken part in their remembrance of Otis. The motel had been transformed from a continual round of in-and-out transits to something like a lodge where people stayed for a while. A concern for their welfare had crept in. But he did not like Sam's tone. He said, "I saw a pack two winters ago, strung out, going someplace, They were looking good." He opened the door with a bang and the door banged again as it closed itself.

Helen shouted, "Sam, this has to stop." Her voice quavered, she struggled for control. "You treat people like an inquisitor. I've had it, I quit."

She was shaking, trying to rise. Maud helped her. Dennis said, "Let's take a break."

Herb closed the meeting. "Get together in the morning."

Sylvie and Maud went with Helen to Helen's unit. Helen collapsed on one of the beds. Maud stretched out on the other; Sylvie took the armchair, knowing she wouldn't stay there long, her left leg was acting up.

Maud said, "Helen, you're going a little bit over the top."

Helen, her eyes closed, said she was sorry, but so worn out, travelling with Sam and Paul, trying to stay calm.

"That's real work, staying calm," Sylvie said. "Try to get some sleep."

"Yes, do that," Maud said, "but there's other work to be done and we want you in on it."

Helen opened her eyes. "I do want to be a part of all this, but not with Sam."

"We'll talk about it, later," Sylvie said.

Herb took it upon himself to invite Paul and Sam to a late supper at Rita's. After some chit chat the Harbor View travellers brought up the pack of Atlantic Fisheries singles they'd brought with them from Malone.

"Don't tell me we've got more door-to-door work," Herb said. "We need some rest."

Sam said, "All we know is Enid Shaw asked us to help out in Malone. We did that, we pitched in."

Paul said. "The sea turtle people up in Maine, they wanted a quality job of printing. There are printers in Malone can do just about anything. That's why the print order ended up there. Then, unbeknownst to us, some Malone lurkers on

Breakout donated some money, upped the print run to 1,500."

"Enid didn't say anything to us about it." Herb said.

"Lemmon anti war," Sam said, "that's maybe the reason. Too much happening all at once. FYI, I'm all for the Lemmon action."

"Sam, we'll get to that," Paul said. "What I want to know is what do we do with this these Atlantic Fisheries singles.

"There's no doubt a nursing home in this town,"Sam said. "We could liberate two or three inmates, get their help." He looked frail, hunched over his fish sandwich, glasses far forward, but he was smiling.

"Let's get serious," Paul said.

"I *am* serious," Sam said.

"Oh Christ," Paul said, "here we go again."

Howie Blake arrived after dark. Herb told him they'd be meeting in the morning, to make plans.

"Sleep is what I need," Howie said.

"A lot's been happening," Herb said. He led Howie to Sam's unit. The room was dark, Sam in bed. Herb apologized, introduced Howie and went away. Howie sat down on the other bed and reached for his shoelaces. "Sorry to disturb you. I'm just another traveler, reporting for duty."

Sam mumbled. "Fugitive from geriatrics?"

"Not quite yet. Freelance keyboard player, hoping to help out in small ways."

"The Lemmon action?"

"And Breakout. It's all tied together."

"I've run into trouble, ever since leaving Harbor View. Spoke out at a big eco-conference in New Hampshire. My companions thought it was a bust, but it wasn't. They don't understand academia."

"I don't either," Howie said. He undressed and got into bed.

Sam wouldn't let go. "Strange subspecies, academics. I'm one of them, and take some pride in that, believe it or not, but I also pride myself on being able to look past professionalism once in a while. History, that's my profession. Dabbled in literature too."

"I see," Howie said.

"Once free of Harbor View I was determined to have a last go at stiff minds, men and women who delight in delicate balancing acts."

Howie, dozing, said, "I see."

"And so, I did speak out, at the question period after the celeb had his turn. There were a few quite passionate counters to my little outburst, which I welcomed. My two colleagues thought I'd been totally routed. Not so. One simply has to throw outrageous-sounding principles into the dull compromise swamp of bland complacency. I chose the right time and the right place. I'm glad. I feel good about it. Helen's hostility, that's another matter. Perhaps I did her wrong, somewhere along the way. I ought to apologize, if only I knew where I went wrong with her."

Howie was asleep.

Next morning, Maud alerted Howie. "Helen Smithson is stranded, alone and distraught. Could you talk to her?"

"Sure. Why me?"

"Because you're driving a truck, all by your lonesome."

He balked, then had to laugh. "Maud, you are the limit."

"It's time we started jumping limits."

"Sure, this loner will talk to another loner. No problem. On one conditon: you keep singing, writing songs."

"Oh Howie, you're so kind."

"No, I mean it. I absolutely do mean it."

Howie found Helen at Rita's, in a corner table far from the windows. She was brooding over toast and coffee.

"Helen? I'm Howie, got in late last night. I'm with Breakout."

She looked him over. "I'm with Breakout too. At least, I was. Now I don't know where I am."

"I'm a little uncertain too."

"How did you know I was Helen?"

"Maud described you."

"Oh, I see. A plot. You are sent, to comfort me."

"No, not comfort. Business. I know you've been driving that Ford Explorer all over the northeast."

"You're wrong. I didn't do any driving, even though I'm a hell of a lot better driver than my male partners. Partners, hah!"

"Would you happen to have a driver's license?"

"What kind of question is that?" But she dug in her pants pocket for her billfold, flipped it open, studied the fine print of her license. "I was interred in Harbor View for barely a year. Before that I was a free citizen, drove my own vehicle. This New Jersey license expires eleven months from now."

"Great, we'll trade off driving, be in New Orleans in three, four days."

"And what would we be doing in New Orleans?"

"We'd be trying to recruit the Swamp Heralds for a big cross-country tour, for Breakout, and Lemmon too. Double bill, so to speak."

"And who supplies the money?"

"Breakout, I hope."

"You hope."

"I thought maybe you could give Enid or Jennifer a call."

Helen looked thoughtful. "You know, Howie, I wouldn't mind doing that."

New Orleans, Louisiana.

Hugo Bogart surveyed his guests, Howie Blake and Helen Smithson. "Who're these two honkies come to see an old has been?" He was speaking deliberately and directly to a young man who stood at the outer doorway.

"Breakout," the young man said.

Howie said, "Pierre sent us."

"Uh huh."

The young man retreated to a position behind Bogart's chair, a shadowed place. The room was lighted by a single lamp on a table at Bogart's right hand, a well-fleshed hand resting there, holding a slender cigar. A big man, dressed in a flowered vest over a bright green shirt, black trousers that had a faint gleam of striping. One cuff was folded neatly over the stump of his left leg. "Set yourselves down. If Pierre sent you, I'm pleased to hear what's on your minds."

Helen and Howie sat on a big chocolate-colored couch. "I know Pierre Lamont," Howie said. "Subbed for him once. Piano. I'd like you to meet my colleague, Helen Smithson. She's a nurse, very smart woman. Pierre said you know about the Lemmon Alliance."

"Glad to meet you miz Smithson, and this here is my nephew, Daryl. He does a few little things around the house I can't get to." He gestured with the cigar to his leg stump. "Vietnam. Me and this lost leg been keepin' company all that time."

Howie said, "Pierre told us you claimed to have gone to 'Nam young, came back old. Hope you don't mind my mentioning that."

Hobart laughed, a low rolling baritome. "Don't mind at all, young man. Wounds ought to be noticed. Because why? Because war has got to be taken note of. I been fighting all these long years, walking away from war on my crutch and one good leg. Korea, that war, forgotten now. Vietnam's going that way. And how about the Philippines, way way back. Nobody knows. American boys in uniform shooting up villages over there. The big-wigs back in Washington called those people 'little brown brothers,' and all the time the U.S.A had their own soldiers shooting whole villages." He turned to Daryl. "You might get these folks something."

Daryl grinned, asked, "Lemonade? Coffee? Tea?"

"Lemonade, please," Helen said.

Howie asked for the same and Bogart said, "You know what I'll have," but Daryl said, "Too early, Uncle," and slipped away.

Helen said, "Mister Bogart…"

He stopped her with a raised hand, ashes sifting down to a big green coiled-viper bowl. "Hugo to you, miz Smithson."

"Thank you, and Helen to you. Now then, Breakout offers to pay full expenses for an extensive road tour if you and the Swamp Heralds agree to feature endangered species material, making it integral to the peace message."

"*Material.* Just what would that be, Helen?"

"Posters, little statements in printed matter, maybe even big pictures on the stage, that sort of thing. Quite a few Breakout people joined the Lemmon effort because they see vital connections between species extinctions and endless wars."

"Ah, I like the sound of that. Keep it up, Helen. Sure, we'll spread species in there all you want. Maybe with your help?"

She turned to Howie, questioning.

He said, "Take it on, Helen. I'll help all I can. So will the amphibian and sea turtle people."

She laughed. "And the black-footed ferret people and the sage grouse people. Okay, I'll do it."

Hobart raised the cigar again. Two conditions: One, I want my new song in there. Didn't Pierre mention that?"

Howie nodded, vigorously, "Yes, he told us about that, and we want it, have to have it."

"And two, we pick a concert to record live. None of this tinkering in a studio. Live recording, all the warts and shouts and whatevers."

Daryl brought lemonade, a split mint leaf on each glass.

Bogard said, "I'll hum you the song, right now. It's dark dark blue, but it doesn't whine. No, we don't whine. The Heralds, we're way out there in the beyond whine. Oh my, I have to tell you, our vocalist, you'll have to hear her, voice like velvet over cold steel."

Daryl switched off the lamp. Helen closed her eyes. Muted New Orleans traffic outside. In the dark duskiness of the room, Bogard's voice.

"It's called *Valley of Malice*."

Brother, did you walk that valley or did you turn
away?
from that valley, sister, rose the cloud.

Hiroshima.
Nagasaki.
Did you turn away?

(Whisker on the drum, sax opens up, horn answers)

I was at the Somme, did you see me there?
Wrapped in barbed wire screaming
bleeding in the rain.

Sister, brother, I was there.
Nanking
Iwo Jima
Riva Ridge
Kaesong

Did you turn away?

(All-brass chaos improvisation, then solo drum)

"Sister did I see you at the midnight revel
ordinance from afar?
Children burning, screaming
Creatures of our kind.
Did youi see the topgun kid, gunning from afar?
Were you in that valley,
did you turn away?

(Long drum solo)

Dying is not quiet, brother,
Dying makes a noise.
Were you watching from afar
shock and awe?
Were you with me in the burning
bodies twisting, crying
creatures of our kind?

(Brasses screech)

Wounded Knee
Sand Creek
Mai Lai
Dying is a blaze

Dying is a sign.

(Brasses screech)

Sisters, brothers, creatures all
do I see you in that valley
did you turn away?

Sisters, brothers, are you there
in mist of blood and malice
or have you turned away?

Daryl turned the lamp on and Hugo grinned at Helen. "Could I offer you a cigar?"

"No, thank you...well, okay, why not?"

Daryl opened a box and offered it to Hugo whose big hand delictely selected two cigars, one for Helen, one for Howie. "They're from Havana."

Howie said, "First order of business, get that song recorded."

"Remember my condition. Swamp Heralds live."

"Hugo, that will be done."

"All right, we've got us an understanding. Now Daryl, get out the branchwater and no back talk."

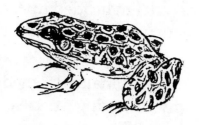

Enid took her stand at the junction of U.S. 30 and Wyoming 34. A stiff cold wind ruffled her sign.

BRING THEM HOME

She wore a sheepskin-lined coat with big pickets and she kept alternate hands stuffed deep into those pockets. Traffic sparse, but each driver slowed nearly to a stop to take in the situation. Surprised curiosity seemed to be the main reaction, but there was one outraged shout, a couple of thumbs down. a few smiles, some of them ambiguous, some not.

A dump truck, turning onto 34, came to a complete and abrupt stop. Enid recogized the driver. She hesitated then gave him a little wave. The driver set the brake and stepped out. "I believe I know you," he said.

"Oh yes, you and your son, master masons. I'm Enid. Enid Shaw."

"Lloyd Morgan. I'm headed up Sybille canyon for a load of fancy stone. What in hell you up to here?"

"Stop war, Lloyd. Finally dawned on me, war gets in the way of saving species. All species, ourselves included. Especially us."

"Well, sure, I guess that's true, but you oughtn't be standing here all by your lonesome."

"I did ask around, in Rock River. One person came close to joining me."

"Jack Lapelle,"Morgan said. He dug into a pocket, came up with a cell phone.

"How on earth did you know?"

Morgan grinned. "Rock River's old hippie. Talks a wild line. Harmless." Loyd punched a number on his phone. "Alice? I'm just east of Bosler, a woman here all by herself with a against war sign. I was wondering if you'd have time to bring her some coffee or something."

He listened, frowning. "No, that's not what I'm asking you to do. For Christ sake, Alice, you know ..."

He listened, his weathered face fixed in deep lines of disapproval. "Yeah, but..." He glanced at Enid, shaking his head.

Enid said, "Please, don't bother."

Morgan, gripped the phone tightly, listened intently, frowned ferociously at nearby mountains. But when he spoke into the phone his voice softened. "You be careful now. I'll be back along here in about an hour and a half." He switched off. "Alice, that's my wife, she says she's coming down here to stand with you."

"I'm sorry, I really am," Enid said. "I didn't want to create trouble. This standing here is something I had to do. Wasn't easy, believe me, but …"

"That's what Alice said. Something she has to do. Damn, wish I'd kept my big mouth shut. She reminded me our son is near military age. That's one thing I don't have to be reminded about." Absently, he put the phone away. "Damn," he said.

Jennifer and Wayne rode double on the hog north through Sybille canyon to where Wyoming 34 met I-25. They were joined a few minutes later by a couple from Wheatland who draped an Old Glory on a shrubby juniper and unfurled a banner.

STUDY WAR NO MORE

Jennifer's and Wayne's sign featured the peace symbol in red on white cardboard and a leaping black-footed ferret.

The wind was pesky, but time passed quickly. The Wheatland couple had a fund of stories from previous demos. "This one's different," they said. "This one is deliciously simple and challenging and democratic."

Jennifer felt that her lonely struggle on these high plains and in these rough mountains, was finding itself in the presence of others, of people who knew something about hands-on effort, people who knew the territory.

At first, in her Medicine Bow life, it had been all about animals, the thrill of being close to deer and antelope, coyotes and badgers, eagles and rattlesnakes and falcons, noticing them with care, taking into herself their notice of her. But the people of Medicine Bow entered that life and then people from elsewhere...Rufus and Wayne and Enid...and now the people from sea to shining sea, standing, showing.

An oil tanker squealed to a full stop, waited on I-25 traffic. The driver rolled down his window and shouted, "Won't do any good."

Jennifer ran to his window, stretched high, handing him a Sage Grouse single. The driver accepted it absently; his look was on her, seizing her with his eyes. "What's a lovely young thing like you doin' out here?"

"Put your eyeballs back in, maybe I'll tell you."

"Well now..." he began, but further words failed to rise. He widened his grin.

"Road's clear," she said. "You can go now."

To: BREAKOUT@LISTSERV.SPEAKUP.ORG

From: jkraus@texoco.com

Re: Standing.

Big posters and banners and people, a great day. Across town in the evening Houston toad defenders put on a hootenanny. Tex-Mex guitars and a vocalist who included in her repertoire a new song, written by Teresa Andrada, activist. The song's title: Toad's Golden Eyes.

Later, the floor was cleared and we danced till two in the morning.

We will plan an even bigger stakeout of all roads into and out of Austin, for the next Saturday Showing. Stand Tall for All, toads too. Jason

Stillwater, Oklahoma.

The Swamp Heralds hosted a raucous, cheerful, alcoholic gathering. Howie and Helen were there. Howie was invited to sit in on the finale featuring Hugo Bogart's new song, rendered dark blue by the Herald's vocalist. Recorded live.

Springfield, Illinois.

The turnout was terrific. On the bandstand paper peace doves hung by threads from the ceiling and moved slowly, sometimes in unison, sometimes not, and a long roll of butcher paper ran across the front of the bandstand, in gold:

WAR KILLS ALL

Dennis called dances until near midnight; Maud sang; Ferguson danced with Jeraldine, one of the organizers; Sylvie and Herb ventured onto the floor for a few waltz steps; Leonard at the entrance offered Indiana Bat singles, fresh off the press.

George ended the party with "Good Night Ladies" on his sentimental fiddle.The hall emptied quickly. Jeraldine and her crew of organizers, happy and energized, gathered around the Breakout travelers to critique the evening and to give thanks. Ferguson turned out the lights and locked the doors and they all drifted across the parking lot into the glare of security lights. Sylvie stopped, Maud bumped into her. "Something's wrong," Sylvie said.

The Breakout bus was there, but its bright paintings of whales and turtles were only partly visible, blocked by a sizeable group of people facing them in silence.

Dennis said, "Bound to happen, sooner or later. I just hope my guitar comes through okay."

Jeraldine turned to Herb. "What's going on?

No answer was required. A middle aged man stepped forward. "Let me introduce myself. Ivan Holbrook." He gestured to his companions. "We're patriots. This is a patriot action. Stay calm, get in your bus, follow us, we'll guide you. This is an interrogation operation. If you have nothing to hide you have nothing to fear."

Maud asked, "You're arresting us?"

A man next to Holbrook leaned forward and pointed angrily toward the Breakout bus. "If you people want action, we're prepared to give it to you. Get on the bus." His colleagues were moving quietly, making a half circle, trapping organizers and Breakout travelers against the wall of Prairie Rose.

Herb said, "You can't do this. You have to charge us with something."

Holbrook said, calmly. "Actually, we can do this. We *are* doing it. America is at war, haven't you noticed? We're prepared to act. Make no mistake about that."

From the darkness of the mass of patriots, a gleam of steel shaped very like a rifle barrel. Ferguson saw it. He knew he had to make a move, the only possible move. He found himself taking two hesitant steps, then one more to within a foot or two of Ivan Holbrook. He said, "We need to talk."

The man jerked back. "No talk, just move it."

"We understand," Ferguson said, "but you need to listen to me first. If you don't you'll be very sorry." His voice went lower, nearly a whisper. "You will be very far up shit creek."

The leader betrayed a hint of uncertainty; one of his hands fumbled with the zipper of his jacket. His nails were manicured, his shirt collar crisp, clean, pressed. Ferguson noticed, recognized the type, Ferguson was of that tribe himself.

Holbrook growled, "Let's cut the chatter."

Ferguson said, "I'm in real estate, Grayling, Michigan, and again I have to ask you for half a minute of private talk, for your own sake. I am a patriot, a minuteman."

"That doesn't impress me. They all say that."

Ferguson flipped out his billfold, extracted a card. "Call this number, my colleague in Grayling. I have a cell phone."

"I have my own," Holbrook saod. He took it from his inner jacket pocket, punched out the number Ferguson held out to him, and waited. Everyone waited, the silence intense. Ferguson had very little hope. Eleven thirty in Grayling. Would gung-ho Gorham answer?

Holbrook held the phone away from his face, listened to it ring and ring and ring. He shook his head. Ferguson pleaded. "Wait, please wait."

The phone squawked. Everyone heard a voice from the phone and judged its tone: sleepy annoyance. Now Holbrook was speaking, then listening, frowning hard, then speaking again, apparently an angry question. Then he subsided, looked hard at Ferguson. He pocketed his phone and turned to his compatriots. "It seems we've run into a serious security situation. I suggest we release these people with a warning."

One of his colleagues spoke up, his voice loud, angry. "Without you telling us what the hell this is all about? No way, Ivan. We're in this together." The speaker was the man with the rifle. He shifted it uneasily, though the muzzle stayed firmly aimed at blacktop.

"All right, Cal," Holbrook replied. "I appreciate that. Gather around, we'll have a minute of private conversation." The man with the rifle obeyed, the others followed. The low-voiced conversation didn't last long. Holbrook turned to the Breakout travelers. "You who are linked to Breakout, we issue you a warning. Do not be fooled into something you might regret later. We advise you to make sure your not being taken for a ride."

"Terrorist ride," Maud said.

"That's the general idea," Holbrook said.

"Total bullshit," Maud said.

Ferguson stood alone, desperately fabricating lies. None of them worked. He watched Holbrook and his patriots step into their vehicles. Headlights swept the place and motors roared. Ferguson feared the silence that would return, and it did, and he walked to his Breakout companions and told the truth, as he saw it and in more detail than necessary, how he had volunterred to join the Breakout travelers, to search for secrets dark and dangerous. "I didn't find anything," he said.

Maud and Sylvie stepped to his side. Maud tapped him on the shoulder. "Thank you, Fergie. You got us out of real trouble."

Sylvie leaned close and whispered. "We knew, about you."

"That I was ...?"

"A spy, yes."

"You all knew?"

"Just Maud and me, I think,"

Ferguson stood there, stunned, looking from one to the other.

Maud said, "We took a chance on you, Fergie, that you wouldn't report lies."

Ferguson said. "I'll go now." He walked away, stumbled once, recovered and went on. Maud called out, "Fergie, get back here"

Ferguson kept on walking, the dark street was about to take him. It was Leonard who trotted to Ferguson, put a firm grip on his shoulder and guided him to the bus, unlocked the door, gave him a little shove and followed him in. The door closed, the motor roared.

"Okay, let's load up," Herb said, and he thanked the organisers who were nearly speachless, wrapped in amazement, and concern, for Breakout, for themselves.

The travellers made their way to the bus and up the steps. They took seats far forward. Ferguson was slumped on the rear bench. Leonard turned out the aisle lights. "Where to?" he asked.

"Interstate," Herb said.

"Which way, Herb? You want Omaha, Chicago, Indianapolis?"

"Let's go home," Dennis said.

"Jonesport?"

"Grayling."

To: BREAKOUT@LISTSERV.SPEAKUP.ORG

From: lyoung@saltaire.com

Re: Lemmon Showing

Nobody going into or out of the greater Salt Lake area could avoid seeing at least one anti-war stand. We got the finger, we got mad shouts and we got smiles and raised fists. International. Airport too, we had that well covered.

Those dull-colored salt flats out there look more friendly to me now. I'm sort of thinking we were reaching out to them too. This is not emotional romanticism by a young thing. I'm a grown woman raising two kids on a single parent income and I've been around if you don't mind my saying so. My stand junction was out there on the edge of the salty vegetation and I swear it's true, that place has a beauty all its own. Go out there sometime, stop, take your time, don't rush away, don't look at your watch, just be there. FYI, peace and respect for the earth is good Mormon doctrine, I am intrigued by a slogan someone sent us: MAHBU, Mormons and Heathens for a Better Utah.

Lilian

Quiet Pines.

As soon as Leonard pulled into the parking area Ferguson went forward and stood in the well. When Leonard opened the door Ferguson hurried away without a word. The others watched him go. No one wanted to stop him. It had been a tough night at the layby outside Decatur, trying to sleep in the roar of diesels, and then the drive to Grayling and Ferguson not speaking. Dennis had tried strumming for a while, singing softlly, but he soon gave it up.

Ferguson and Marie sat up late. He wanted sympathy and didn't get it. She wanted an apology, and didn't get that.

Marie, exasperated, brought out a bottle of California Pinot Noir. She poured. "Let's start over." She twirled her glass, sipped, sipped again. "You're telling me, in all this time you've been traveling all over hell and gone with those folks, and knocking on doors with those animal papers…you didn't find out anything."

"They're not terrorists."

"Harmless old people."

"Some old, really old; some not. I'm not saying they're harmless. Hell, they're capable of quite a lot of things, actually. Besides, who's to say what's harmless and what's not. I'm trying to tell you, Marie, this world is more complicated than we ever thought."

"I know that."

He looked at her. "I suppose maybe you do."

"Let's put this all behind us, get back to business." She tipped her glass toward his.

He told himself to forget Maud and Sylvie and Babs, Otis and Herb and Leonard, George and Dennis and Howie. And all the fervid folks he'd met, out there on the highways and byways. And the whale and the sea turtle singles. Loosen up, Al, it's going to be great, getting back in the groove that's really yours, where you can be yourself. Besides, there'll be some good stories to tell.

Where would he tell the stories, without betrayal, anoher betrayal? He saw it now, the misery of it, the impossibility. He couldn't put it behind him. He managed a smile for Marie.

To: BREAKOUT@LISTSERV.SPEAKUP.ORG

From: cbiochi@aol.com:

Re: Eels

Latest reports about eels in the Great Lakes is devastating. There used to be a thriving eel fishery, tons of eels caught each year. Finally the Ontario government ordered the fishery closed (what was left of it) because there are so few eels left. Should have done that earlier, but that would have taken political courage. We don't have that. Maybe we never did.

Somewhat sad in Kingston, Ontario, Canada.

To: BREAKOUT@LISTSERV.SPEAKOUT.ORG

From: kromig@coastal.com

Re: stubborn toad

John Roberts, as a Circuit Court judge, dissenting, went against the arroyo toad, writing that "for reasons of its own [the toad] lives its entire life in California." Therefore, he concluded, it is of no federal concern.

Hey John, look it up: Endangered Species Act.

Grayling, Michigan.

George and Dennis, strolling on a back sreet talking about the coasts of Maine. They were homesick.

"We're family men," Dennis said.

George said, "You don't have to keep saying that." He stopped and pointed. "Am I seeing things?"

Dennis looked. A man was conversing with another man, on the tiny front porch of a modern single level house. "Ferguson. Back to the old grind. Real estate, door-to-door."

"The least we can do is say hello."

Ferguson was crossing the lawn now. He came to the street, noticed George and Dennis. For a couple of blinks he tried to pretend he hadn't. Giving that up, he tried a half-hearted wave and walked on, but they hustled, cut him off at the intersection. George said, "How you doing, Al?"

"Okay. How's everybody?"

"None of us gettin' any younger," Dennis said.

"That's for sure," Ferguson said.

"Look, Al," George said, "we don't hold a grudge. It took real guts for you to bail us out, in Springfield."

"I'm not proud of any of that." He kept fussing with a bundle of papers that was tucked under his left arm.

Dennis said, "Stop in at Quiet Pines, sometime real soon. Boshardt set up a couple of those new coffee makers in the office. Keeps them going all day. We drop in any time we want, have a cup. Free. Don't know what got into him, he's such a tightwad, not that I blame him, it's been a rough road for him. How's *your* business?"

"Not bad. Actually, Marie is taking over a good part of it, doing really well. Gives me a little spare time, for other things."

By now, George and Dennis were both staring hard and pointedly at the bundle of paper Ferguson held tightly under his left arm. Why did he keep fussing with them? Trying to hide something?

Ferguson said, "Nice seeing you guys."

Dennis shook his head, smiling. "Like old times, eh? Door-to-door. Looks like heavy duty paper you got there. Strikes me as kind of familiar."

Ferguson gave up. He handed a sheet to George, another to Dennis.

George asked, "What is it?"

"Pallid sturgeon. Endangered."

George and Dennis examined the sheet, admiring the sturgeon lunging across the top of the sheet, backed by a ragged splash of bright blue.

Ferguson said, "When we were doing turtle sheets I met an old guy who used to do clip art. He did the sturgeon. I paid him for it."

"Lovely job," George said.

Dennis said. "I don't know damn all about sturgeons. Freshwater?"

"Mississippi drainage," Ferguson said. "Well, I better get on, finish up these." He lifted the singles, helplessly.

"Come on, Al, hand over a few. We'll do this batch in no time." Dennis was looking Ferguson straight between the eyes, a blue-eyed lock. "Al, we need you."

"Enough chit-chat," George said, "let's get to work."

Lemmon, South Dakota

Rufus called Enid. "How did it go?"

"Not sure yet. I made a new friend, a woman who came out to stand with me. Jennifer and Wayne and another couple took a stand also, further north from me. The Star Trib did a decent reporting job. Apparently there was a counter-demo in the Casper area and some shouting and shoving. One person in Rock River scolded me for taking part, but another took me aside and said he was proud of me. I asked him if he'd go with me to the next showing and he just stared at me. I told him there would be more of those. He told me maybe he'd wear a ski mask so his boss wouldn't recognize him. We both laughed at that. I said, "Don't you dare." He went away thoughtful. What do you make of that?"

"I think you're organizing Wyoming."

"No such thing. My arrogance doesn't stretch that far. How did it go in South Dakota?"

"News is slow filtering in. Some hassling, some arrests. General impression is that quite a few people turned out. Reason I'm calling is we've got problems up here. Maureen and I are doing what we can, but the organizers, these three women, they're burned out, need a break."

"Maureen? Name doesn't ring a bell."

"Oh, uh, we met in Chadron, Nebraska. She's a great organizer. You'd like her. We came up here, found an apartment for rent. Anyway, the scene here, you wouldn't believe. Over a hundred affiliated outfits sending in questions and ideas and complaints and we've got only two computers and two phones all jammed into the back rooms of The Hair Affair. Maureen's helping out there, but Gretchen had to hire an extra hair worker who's not experienced, so what with dealing with customers and the rest of the United States, and some from Canada too. I don't know how Gretchen keeps going. None of these women are spring chickens."

"Rufus, you're engaged."

"Engaged? No, not really. Maureen and I, we struck up a friendship , in Chadron …"

"Oh silly me, I mean, *engaged* as in *excited*, totally *committed*."

"Oh sure, mainly being a gofer. Enid, the important thing is, these people need phones and computers and printers and a bigger working space."

"And money."

"Yes, that would help."

"You and Maureen are on the ground there. Send me a detailed list of needs. Very specific specs, because I'm not a technical person. Oh, and do you think the Breakout bus people might want to lend a hand?"

"A dance would be just the right thing here, to break the ice. Believe me, there is ice."

"I'm sure there is. I know about ice."

Quiet Pines.

Herb called another conference, in the new meeting place behind Quiet Pines. "Do we put on a dance in Lemmon?"

It was decided quickly. Yes.

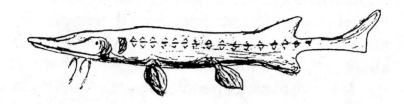

Grayling.

Sam and Paul, left behind with nearly a hundred Atlantic Fisheries singles, stood in the motel parking lot, waved, tried to look cheerful as the Breakout travelers headed out. Then they went back to work.

As in Malone, Sam recognized a hard fact: Paul was better at doorstep conversation, he had the touch, listening intently, inserting his remarks deftly and, above all, not falling into the lofty lecture mode that nearly always captured Sam.

But Sam was doing his best, adapting, taking in data.

From the man on his day off, angry, impatient, a million things to take care of, no time for the fisheries crisis.

From the nostalgic woman who had once lived near an ocean beach. She would read about barn door skates and other sea creatures later. Behind her, a huge parrot in a cage, cocking its head at Sam.

From the high school kid who was on his way to a part-time job, informing Sam that he already knew about ecosystems, and so what? He was about to list up with the Marines. "A job, that's all it is. If I have to shoot people, well, part of the job. If I get killed, part of the job. You got choices, maybe? I don't."

From the woman in robe and slippers who told him she'd read the "propaganda" if he'd take her husband's dog to the vet. Otherwise, bug off.

From people rushing away, leaving behind the aged, the unemployed, the cats and dogs. Notes on doors, advising a family member when another family member would be back, or giving instructions: groceries, detergent, fuel for the lawnmower, pizza, beer.

From an astonishingly young babysitter, curious and attentive. "Thank you, I'll read it. Have a good day."

Sam, in his eighth decade, did notice these things. Selectively, yes, like everyone else, but he was a scholar, after all, trained to bear down hard on whatever needed scrutiny. Now, door-to-door in Grayling, limping and lurching, pain in shoulders and knees, blurry-eyed because he needed a new prescription, Sam blundered on.

Next house. A child on threadbare persian rug gnawing vigorously on a plastic H from its alphabet set.

There was a time when Sam's post-modern mind would have happily formed a metaphor: Child eating language, topic for the next analysis, perhaps for next meeting of the Modern Language Association. But now, watching the astoundingly copious flow of saliva, and the cihild's calm and steady stare, metaphor failed.

Next house, another door, another opening, a man in black-rimmed spectacles holding a NY Times. "Aha, heard about you people. Peddling endangered species, right?"

"Information," Sam began, but the man was standing back, beckoning. "Come in, we'll discuss it."

P aul, behind the Explorer's wheel, fretted. He had to pee and where the hell was Sam? He drove down the street. There he was, hurrying down the sidewalk. Paul honked and stopped. Sam climbed in. "Got to pee."

Paul found Main street, parked at Don's Subway. They sat at a small table. It was high noon. They were exhausted. Sam said, "That last house, the guy invited me in. I couldn't very well refuse. The whole idea is to engage in conversation."

"Conversation, yes, lectures no."

"I know what you think of me, Paul. Anyway, this guy was the one doing the lecturing. Talked a blue streak. Turned out he knows all about Breakout and all about California condors, absolutely all of what's going on in California. Lead poisoning, latest prob for condors. Condors are scavengers, pick up bullet lead from animals killed by hunters."

"I know that."

"He got into those Dan Diego scandals. Amazing the things we don't hear about. Enviros thought they had an agreement to save extremely endangered species. But no, bulldozers were in charge."

Paul sighed. "Save San Diego for later. You know, I've been thinking, here we are living off Breakout's per diem and what have we actually accomplished for them?"

"We raised hell up in New Hampshire."

"Fifteen minutes of harangue and humiliation."

"I know how you and Helen feel about it. Do we have to go over it again?"

"No, we sure as hell don't."

"I talk too much. I realize that."

"Talking too much, that's not really it. You don't make allowances, Sam; that's the problem, in my humble opinion."

"Allowances?"

"Yeah, allowances, for the person you're lecturing at. Where they are, what their situation in life is. You've got no more diplomacy than a chipmunk."

"Better than being two-faced. Better than straddling fences your whole life."

"You think I've spent my life straddling fences?"

"I didn't mean you. You're bold enough, in a diplomatic sort of way."

"Enough about us," Paul said.

Sam noticed a woman in baggy pants and sleeveless shirt who was tending a very young child. An older child picked at her half sub. Sam remembered the slobbering kid on the Persian rug, gnawing an H. Faces passed in review, people he'd met that morning and the morning before. He saw no special marks of heroism in those faces. Instead, a terrible intensity. People, my own species. California condor man. The polite baby sitter. The exasperated woman with the dog. The woman with the parrot. People.

Helen, Paul, Harvey Boshardt…Dennis and George. Herb, Sylvie, Maud, Ferguson…Sam. His mind, ticking away in scholarly fashion, suddenly went blank, making way for the simple realization that behind the frustrations of door-to-door, and the boredom, there had been a smidgeon of enjoyment. Fun? Well, yes.

Paul said, "I just now thought of how we can do some work for Breakout, pay for our keep, so to speak. How do you feel about this Lemmon Alliance Stop War move?"

"In theory, I'm in favor of any anti war stance."

Paul growled, "Never mind theory. Will you stand up for it?"

"Stand up? What are you getting at?"

"I'm getting at us standing up here, now, telling this crowd that we are anti-war people and we'll be outside to talk to anybody who wants to take action."

Sam said, "All right."

Paul looked at him in surprise. "I expected you to talk the idea to death."

Sam smiled. "You go first, this side of the room. I'll follow your lead, on the other side."

P aul stood up. "I'll ask for fifteen seconds of their attention. I'll say that anybody interested in stopping war meet us outside at the Ford Explorer. That's all. No speeches. I'm serious, Sam."

Sam made a little bow. "Like I said, I'll follow your lead."

P aul and Sam, in the Ford, dozing. A sharp tap on the hood. A woman wearing a white and red headscarf and brown cotton shirt and trousers stood disapprovingly at the driver's window. She said, "Are you guys serious?"

A teenage couple appeared in the parking lot, noticed Pearl talking to men they recognized as the two geezers who had called their attention to something called *Lemmon*. A little curious, they walked toward the Explorer and listened. Pearl beckoned them closer. "This is important," she said. "Do you know about war?"

The young woman laughed and in an antsy high-pitched voice told Pearl that every American knows about war.

Pearl said, "No. Every American does not know about war. My nephew was in the infantry, killed in action. Friendly fire. And for what? Now then, let's get organized. I'll arrange a meeting place. Tomorrow evening?" She turned to Paul and Sam. "Seven sharp?"

They, stunned, nodded. The young man took the young woman's arm. "Come on, Tammy, we've heard enough."

Tammy stayed put. "Just a minute, Jer."

Pearl spoke to the young man. "I'm Pearl Braddock. I work at Grayling Dry Cleaners. And you're Jer? This is a special occasion, the five of us meeting like this."

Pearl had already decided on a possible meeting place, and knew that she could count on two friends with whom she had shared gossip, grief and towering anger. But she had her doubts about the two aged gentlemen in the Explorer. She turned to them. "We can meet tomorrow night. Basement of the library is available, I'm pretty sure. I'll check that out. Let's exchange phone numbers. Anybody have a piece of paper?"

Paul handed her a Northeast Fisheries single.

"We're with Breakout," he said, "supporters of Lemmon Alliance."

"Yes, good," Pearl said, hardly glancing at the lively barn door skate that headed the text. She wrote her phone number, handed over to

Tammy and Jer, but Jer wasn't buying. "Come on, Tammy." He tugged at her.

She resisted. She said, "I'll see you later, tonight."

But he stayed. Pearl smiled brightly. "Just a few good men, a few good women, that's all we need, to begin. Tomorrow then, seven, at the library." She handed the fisheries sheet to Tammy.

"Nice fish," Tammy said as she wrote her phone number.

Seven o'clock on the dot, Pearl opened the meeting. "I believe everyone here is acquainted with the Lemmon Alliance and its proposal. Are there any questions?"

There were. Questions and discussion. Five men and two women in uniform entered the room. National Guard. Pearl cut short the discussion, introduced Samuel Horne, PhD, a spokesperson for Breakout.

Sam stood and confessed that he was a fervent believer in activism. A nudge from Paul warned him: cut to the chase. That broke Sam's rhythm. Confused, he noticed the seven in uniform, and that they were about to make a move. He said, "I've been in the military, one of the forgotten wars, but haven't seen combat. I hope there are veterans here who can speak about that, with authority. Let's have a moment of silence, now, remembering those who did not return home."

The moment passed. Sam sat down. Paul nudged him, whispered, "You done good."

There was a combat veteran present, but not from the ranks of those in uniform. Instead, Adrian Balous. Sam recognized him, the California condor man. "Combat," he said, "is not like in the movies. It's not like on TV. It's not easy to talk about. I do want to say that I've come to the conclusion that there is something important we humans can do, for our own survival. Stop killing each other. Stop mindless killing. Please, I have to tell you again, war is not like in the movies, it is not like in recruiting posters. It is a kind of hell, and it is...please, I have to say this...terrible as war is, it also has spells of being pretty damn silly."

A Guardsman spoke up. "We have the right and the duty to protect ourselves against enemies, against terrorists."

"I agree with that," Balou said. "People in uniform here, people not in uniform, we are all citizens of a great country and our duty is to figure out how best to protect ourselves."

A young woman stood and lifted a cardboard sign. "We need good signs," she said, "not floppy poster boards on sticks. I built a better one and here it is."

A Guardsman, one of the women, shouted. "We're at war. Don't you understand? We have to fight, there's no other way out of this." Her comrades backed her with shouts. They tried a hand-clapping routine, but that died and there followed, among everyone, a very few moments of irresolution. Pearl seized it. "Dorothy, could you hold up your sign again? Turn it all the way around so everybody can see the construction."

Dorothy complied

A man stood, holding his hand high and with calm assurance. "I volunteer to let the mayor know what we plan to do."

"And the National Guard?" someone asked.

Adrian Balou said, "I'll inform the Guard."

A woman sprang up. "Let's have a sign making party. Tomorrow?"

"Where?" Pearl demanded.

"Meet at the station, seven o'clock. I'll find us a place."

A young man said, "Make it eight o'clock. I've got kids."

Pearl announced, "Eight it is. Anything else?"

Someone shouted, "Pearl, I love this. We're not using up the whole evening. I can still catch my program."

Applause.

Driving back to Quiet Pines, Paul crowed. "Hey, Sam, look what we started. I can't believe it."

"Pearl's the one pulled it off."

"I realize that. Wonder where she picked up all that know-how. God but I'm tired. Sometimes when I get like this, sleep eternal has a great appeal. You ever feel that way?"

"Oh sure. Right now just a night's sleep will do me."

Wyoming toad and sage grouse people, meeting in the back room of Scents of Sage boutique, decided to not go all out for the Lemmon campaign. Cerise and Jeanne dissented and went home and gloomed for a while. Then they called a friend in Cheyenne. They got together, made plans.

Colorado toad people put Lemmon on hold, decided to wait, see what happens.

To: BREAKOUT@LISTSERV.SPEAKUP.ORG

From: annbr@wyoming.com

Re: War stand

I am a rural mail carrier, that means I'm a federal employee. Don't know if I can legally stand somewhere with a sign. Don't know if I have the nerve anyway.

anna

To: annbr@wyoming.com

From: csant@blissnet.com

Re: War stand

You have every right to stand. Why don't you join us tomorrow? Meet ahead of time in Laramie, at McDonald's? We will be wearing Wilderness Watch shirts.

Cerise

To: eshaw@wyoming.com

From: Helsmith@upsouth.com

Re: Swamp Heralds

Enid, I can't thank you enough for supporting me and my troubles, and for financing the Swamp Heralds. I've taken it upon myself to insure that species continue to get noticed. Also do dogsbody work, and that's okay. This old body has a little life left.   love, Helen

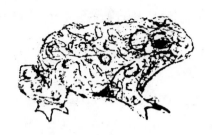

Lemmon, South Dakota.

Rufus limped from *The Hair Affair*, feeling his age and casting back, way back, to a day in the Catskills, he and Otis, vigorous middle-aged men enthralled by birds in the wild, the never-ending challenges. They had followed a creek to its very beginning, a little swampy place hidden in a crease in the hillside. There, listening to the non-stop preaching of a red-eyed vireo, they had talked about their passionate hobby that was more than a hobby. What, then, was it? They couldn't nail it down. They never did.

A man in paint-smeared overalls stepped out of a pickup. "Hey, you're that man from Breakout?"

It took Rufus all of five or six seconds to come back from the Catskills, the long years passing, rolling across the huge continent. "Yes," he said, "that's me."

"I don't like what you're doing. I don't like it one bit."

Rufus nodded.

"We're all patriots here," the man said.

Rufus nodded again, pawed at his chin. His challenger was middle-aged, clean-shaven, his eyes squinted, his lips a thin hard line.

"Uh," Rufus said, "we're all patriots. You got that right."

"Hey, don't give me that liberal bullshit. I'm telling you, this town is true blue American. We support our troops wherever they have to go, whatever they have to do."

Rufus simply stared, at a loss for words.

"Aw shit," the man said." You're too old to know what I'm talking about. Never mind, I've got to get back to work."

That old buried anger surged, the war thing, hot words forming, but Rufus held them back. He asked, "What kind of work are you in?"

"Contracting, whatever needs doing. I have three men working for me over there. He shrugged toward the big building across the street. "Remodeling job. What's it to you?"

"Curiosity. What goes on in there?"

"Wheeler. Big oufit. They make jewelry, Dakota Gold is one of their lines. Sells all over the world, employs a lot of people."

"I didn't know that," Rufus said.

The contractor reached into the bed of the pickup, lifted out a pair of gallon cans of paint. "You got my message? You and that bus load of stop war people? We got our own ideas of what's right." He started to cross the street. Rufus went with him. They walked side by side. The contractor couldn't do anything about that, other than slugging the pesky old fart. Rufus did all the talking. "Here's the inside story about the bus that's headed your way. It will have sea turtles and a whale painted on it, and, I think, a sharp-tailed grouse. The people in the bus have been going around the country handing out information about endangered species. Whales and salmon and prairie dogs and the others, hundreds of others on the verge of extinction. They will put on a dance, maybe two. Outside, if the weather holds."

They reached the other side of the street. The contractor said, "I'm a working man, can't stand around talking all day."

"I understand that," Rufus said, "but I'm giving you inside facts. You want to know, don't you? Two old women will be in the bus. Not quite as old as me, but pretty well along, and one old man. They used to be in a nursing home, decided to get back in the world. Also, the driver, and two fishermen who are alsomusicians, from the state of Maine, and a pianist, I don't know where' he's from. Maybe one or two others. That's it, that's your bus load."

The conractor put the cans on the sidewalk and pointed a hard finger at Rufus. "Dancing is one thing, hooking up with this stop war movement is a whole different ball game."

Rufus stabbed back. "No, same ball game. Animals besides ourselves deserve a little respect; they're on this planet with us; We're in it, for beter or worse, together. Some aimals dance, you know. Like, sharp tailed grouse. Some of them sing. Same game."

The contractor picked up his paint. "I haven't got time for this. I'm telling you, bear in mind what I'm saying, we won't put up with strangers taking over our town."

"Okay," Rufus said, "I promse you, we won't take over the town."

He came to Alex Lee's auto repair with a message and some papers for Sharon, from Gretchen. Today, as usual, Sharon's inside door was open to the repair area. Two hoists, three benches and crowds of equipment. Rufus stepped in there to have a few words with Hans and Rocky. Rocky was young and happily friendly, Hans much more reserved.

Alex yelled from the back bench. "Rufus, I hear you know about birds."

"Some. I'm mainly a math teacher." He stepped with care to Alex's bench, avoiding tires, inner tubes, welding rack, et cetera.

Alex said, "Yeah, I hear that too. Anyway, yesterday I was towing a wreck from Linquist's place, saw a flock of birds, like sparrows, but something funny about them."

Rufus said, "I'm not up on western birds, but I'd like to take a look."

"We close up at 5 o'clock. How about you and me drive out there?"

"Sure. Most likely I'll be at Terrie's or Gretchen's."

At a little after five Alex picked Rufus up at Terrie's. They drove toward the river, slowly. "This is where they were, yesterday," Alex said. "I don't see any."

"Birds move around a lot," Rufus said.

They drove on. "There," Rufus said.

Alex stopped the car. The birds were on the ground, scrounging. Rufus rolled down his window and glassed them. Sparrow-like. Brown striping on the back, white outer tail feathers, but the bill was slender, less stubby than typical sparrows. That ruled out vesper sparrow. Rufus saw one of them dip its tail. He turned to Alex with a big grin, offering the binocs. "Sprague's pipit."

Alex grinned back. "You sound like you struck gold." He accepted the binocs, tried to get a fix on one of the pipits. "Damn nervous rascals."

"Birds tend to be that way," Rufus said.

Alex kept trying, finally caught one. "Whoa, where the hell'd you go?" He persisted, another bird appeared in the visual field. Alex gripped the binocs so hard he had trouble focusing. "Got you, by god," he said, and returned the binocs to Rufus. "Beautiful piece of equipment."

Rufus felt vaguely disappointed.

Alex said, "This species thing, tell me about that."

Rufus told him.

Alex reached to the ignition, hesitated.

"Go ahead," Rufus said. "Out with it."

"Those women didn't think it through. They've gone off half-cocked, started this stop war movement, didn't look ahead, didn't see there'd be a backlash, here on home ground, all kinds of complications."

"They know it now," Rufus said.

"Do they? Well, it doesn't help me any. Hans, my top mechanic, threatens to quit, and a couple important local business people have had a quiet little talk with me, worried about this busload of strangers moving in on us. And they want me to fire Sharon."

"You can't do that."

"You think I don't I know that?"

"Is there any way I could help?"

"I doubt it, except calling off that bus."

"Dammit, Alex, you asked me out here to see these pipits that you don't really give a damn about, to get me to cancel the bus? All I've got to say to you is, you've got me figured wrong."

Alex turned an anguished face to Rufus. "*I was really curious* about the birds. Believe me. Oh hell yes, I wanted to talk, sure I did. You're a stranger, you'll be moving on, I can be honest with you."

Rufus chuckled.

Alex said, "Yeah, I know, what I just said, that's stupid."

They sat there, looking through the windshield at grassland that went in long sweeps of yellows, browns and still a few greens toward the Grand river. Rufus said, "Maybe the drouth is ending."

"Wheat looks good so far, all through the Dakotas. Have to wait and see."

"I spoke to one of your Lemmon citizens earlier today, tried to tell him dancing and respecting other lives on earth go together. I can't prove that, don't really know how to talk about it, but Alex, listen to me.

You tell your business pals that Breakout bus everybody's so up tight about would like very much to put on a dance or two. And that's it, except for a little nudging about endangered species. I have faith in Lemmon. Democracy will survive."

Silence, except for wind teasing the grass.

Alex sighed, turned the ignition key. The motor started, beautifully tuned. "One thing for sure, Rufus, I won't stand for people telling me how to run my business, how to treat the people who work for me."

They rode toward town. Alex said, "I'll have to talk this whole thing over with my wife. So happens, she loves to dance. Might be we'll show up."

Rufus remembered that Maureen had dragged Otis onto the floor and the music took over. He said, "I might show up too."

To: BREAKOUT@LISTSERV.SPEAKUP.ORG

From: annbr@wyoming.com

Re: Standing

Five of us at the junction of 287 and I-80. One of the ranchers I'd talked to about Zapus came along and stopped and talked a while, backing up traffic. He didn't care, asked me why I put a picture of a jumping mouse on my sign. I said it meant saving species went with stopping war. He said he wasn't an environmentalist. I said I wasn't either. He laughed and asked me what I was doing with that Zapus on my sign if I wasn't an enviironmentalist, and I said maybe it was time for us people who weren't environmentalists to get out of their pickup cabs and save some species. He laughed but then looked sort of serious, almost sad. actually. He said there were times when he felt mad enough to do some crazy thing like that.

Anna

Most prairie dogs in modern times live in small colonies. North of Mexico the miles-long settlements of at-risk blacktailed prairie dogs, *Cynomys ludovicianus*, persist only as unverifiable legends.

In August, Jennifer Felway and her two colleagues from Sybille Laboratory released three of their carefully raised black-footed ferrets into a cold and sparkling night in South Dakota. Here was the largest dog town any of them had ever seen. They settled into their sleeping bags, speaking in slow, low tones, watching stars. A mild wind kept mosquitoes down.

Lisa, ethologist, monitored the ferrets' radio collar signals. So far, so good. Steve, physiologist, spoke of the marvelous adaptability of the mammalian body. Jennifer and Lisa had heard it all before, but they didn't mind; they were believers; they had a deep faith in immune systems, in brain flexibility, in the drive and play of muscle, tendon and nerve.

At a little before dawn one of the ferrets, Number 48, a female, roused herself and ventured forth from an empty burrow.

She nosed the air for a while, evaluating again the disturbing smells emanating from unfamiliar leafy things. The feel of the sandy soil under the pads of her feet, and its scent, these too were unfamiliar. And the wind brought strange odors from unseen places.

Mingling in this challenging medley came faintly familiar odors. She moved, searching for their source, found three creatures asleep on the ground. She paused, seeing for the first time their full outstretched size. She investigated, gave the radio a passing sniff, nosed her way along the fabrics, her belly grazing the ground, to each face where she felt on her own black-masked face, warm animal breath.